# AFFINITY

## A SOULFUL HEARTS NOVELLA

TIGRIS EDEN

## CONTENTS

*Synopsis* — vii

Chapter 1 — 1
Chapter 2 — 18
Chapter 3 — 34
Chapter 4 — 44
Chapter 5 — 64
Chapter 6 — 81
Chapter 7 — 84
Chapter 8 — 109
Chapter 9 — 120
Chapter 10 — 133
Chapter 11 — 144
Epilogue — 159

*Thank You for Reading* — 165
*Up Next: Consumed* — 167
*About the Author* — 177
*Other Titles by Tigris Eden* — 179
*Praise for the Shadow Unit Series* — 181
*Praise for Arctic Bound* — 185
*Praise for Diamond* — 187

Affinity © 2019 Tigris Eden

Copyright notice: All rights reserved under the International and Pan-American Copyright Conventions. No part of this book may be reproduced or transmitted in any form or by any means, electronic or mechanical, including photocopying, recording, or by any information storage and retrieval system, without permission in writing from the publisher.

This is a work of fiction. Names, places, characters and incidents are either the product of the author's imagination or are used fictitiously, and any resemblance to any actual persons, living or dead, organizations, events or locales is entirely coincidental.

Warning: the unauthorized reproduction or distribution of this copyrighted work is illegal. Criminal copyright infringement, including infringement without monetary gain, is investigated by the FBI and is punishable by up to 5 years in prison and a fine of $250,000.

Kats Kreative Ideas | Houston, Texas
admin@tigriseden.net | www.tigriseden.com

*To you who really sees me as I am. Regardless of the good and the bad times, it has been you who has stayed by my side. Thank you. And to the members of Eden's Den.*

SYNOPSIS

Special Agent Jada Alexander has a great life working for the ATF's S.E.E.K. unit, but she wishes her nights were filled with more than just Netflix marathons with her fur babies. She yearns for companionship, and while her quirks and fandoms keep her utterly entertained, it's not the same as having someone to come home to.

When a blast from her past comes back into Jada's life, she's thrown for a loop, especially when both Dali and Poe act nothing like the dog and cat she's come to know and love. They immediately accept the irresistible Nicklaus, and she begins to wonder if she has found her soul mate, her very own Viking god to warm her dark nights.

Until Klaus shatters her heart and tells her that he

only wants her as a friend, that he's not ready for a relationship. The problem…she's already half in love with him, and now their lives are so intertwined, she might lose more than just the guy she was hoping to have forever with. She may lose all of her friends from Dallas Fire and Rescue, as well.

Jada's life becomes much like the movies and songs constantly cycling through her head, but the question is, will she get her happily ever after with the matching ballad soundtrack, or will it be a tragedy with a death metal score?

# 1

"RAISE YOUR MUTHAFUCKIN' GLASS TO THE ONE, THE ONLY, MY GIRL, JADA ALEXANDER!"

Caroline, my best friend since childhood, is screaming at the top of her lungs. She's standing on top of the bar, her shot glass raised, and somehow, she's more sober than I am. She's managed twelve, count them *twelve* tequila shots. I'm a lightweight by nature and stopped drinking after the first round. I'm celebrating—quietly, I might add—until Caroline thinks it's a grand idea to start telling everyone, and I mean *everyone* at the bar that I need to get laid.

Fuck my life.

"Wait! Wait," my best friend shouts. Her hands wave wildly, and what alcohol is in her shot glass splashes on the bar and me. I look down at the table, shaking my head.

"Wait up, hold on! Correction!" she yells. "Raise your muthafuckin' glass to the one, the only, *Special Agent* Jada Alexander, ATF's newest S.E.E.K. graduate!"

Caroline screams, yes, screams this information out into the crowd. *This is my life*. I starting to look forward to leaving Sulphur, Louisiana. Gateway to the Creole Nature Trail All-American Road, with a side of Sabine National Wildlife. I like to think of Sulphur as the gateway to hell.

My father agrees with me on that. He's ex-military, and the only man I've ever loved. Okay, there was Jaden, but he's a nasty piece of work. And back then, I sorely lacked in the self-esteem department. I'm two years sober of the man, and drama free. I got my shit together and saw the sleaze for what he was. An emotional and mental abuser.

"Stand up girl, take a bow. Let them see what could be the greatest lay of their life!" Caroline hollers.

"All right, you've had enough. It's time to leave," I advise.

I stand and try to maneuver around the barstool. Let the record show, I'm never clumsy. Like, *ever*. My life is a series of straight lines, right turns, and no curves. I tried that once, jumped on the wild ride of what people deem my shining moment. It's not. It was my worst because I ended up with Jaden. *Never again,* I vow. I don't crave the attention or the extra flare. Give me a book and my two fur babies curled next to me, and all is right in my world.

When I stumble, I don't just try to catch myself before I ass-plant onto the dirty-ass floor, nope, I fall into the strong arms of a stranger. I know he's a stranger because I cased the entire bar at least three times. I always pay close attention to my surroundings.

There are cords and cords of muscle wrapped around my waist, and a tribal tattoo on an arm that goes all the way to a manly wrist. The other arm is bare and free of ink. The stranger's fingernails are black from oil, and my mind supplies his occupation.

Mechanic.

"You all right?"

My body freezes. He has an accent. His r's roll in such a way, I shiver involuntarily. *Please let him be ugly, unattractive, a gazillion worts all over his face. Please, please, please.* I internally chant.

"Jada!"

Great. Caroline. She's screaming my name over

the noise in the bar like a child who's lost their mother.

I still haven't looked up at my would-be rescuer. Truth be told, I'm scared. His hands gently steady me, and he scoots past with a polite, "Excuse me." I could listen to his voice for hours. As he walks through the crowd, I catch a glimpse of his retreating form. Everything, and I mean everything, I see is ah-mazing. If his front looks half as good as his back, I'm a goner. My previous take on abstinence will fly right out the door.

"Jada! Honey, come back and do some shots with us. I see your future ex-baby daddy right here." She points to one of the guys we went to school with. Everett Mullins. That would be a big hell no. He's all right, but he isn't my type. After my last relationship, I don't think anybody is my type. My ex, whose name shall never be mentioned or thought of again, is an asshat. Controlling, bad-tempered, and an all-around creepo.

"Don't want a future anything, Caroline. What I do want is to go home," I yell back. Someone who's clearly had too much to drink boos at me.

"Ah, pooh. You're being a party pooper."

Caroline jumps down from the bar, and the guys join in as she makes faces at me and proceeds to pout and complain. I love her, but I want to be more than just awake for my drive to Dallas tomorrow. Good thing we took separate cars. Dali and Poe are spending the night with my aunt and uncle, who live in Houston. I know my fur babies miss me. I miss them, too.

Caroline pulls me in for a hug.

"I'm gonna miss you, Jada girl. So much."

"Well, come see me in a few weeks," I say, hugging her back.

"You bet your sweet ass I will."

Don't I know it.

We walk out to our cars, and I realize I don't have my keys. I also make sure Jada calls an Uber. Her drunk ass isn't driving anywhere.

"Go ahead, Cara. Call an Uber. I gotta find my keys."

"All right. Text me when you get to the hotel."

"Will do."

A few minutes have passed, and still I can't find my keys. I don't carry a big purse, so I know I must have dropped them somewhere. By the time I'm done searching the parking lot of the bar, Caroline's Uber has arrived.

I watch as she gets into and the back and drives off. The taillights dim in the darkness before I turn around. I never make it into the bar. My keys are dangling in front of me, in the hands of the accented male.

"You dropped your keys."

I'm speechless.

My tongue is ten times its normal size and gets stuck in my mouth.

I'm just plain mesmerized.

He is fucking beautiful. Eye candy to be sure, and he's staring straight at me with my keys in his hand. *For the love of the old gods and the new*. Please let him be real. Don't let this be one of those moments where he looks good in the dark but is bum fuck ugly once the lights are on. *Manners, Jada, manners*, I scold myself.

"Um. Thanks?"

It comes out more of a question than an actual "Thanks." Why doesn't the ground just swallow me whole? Please! Right the fuck now; just kill me. He's at least nice enough to not call me out on my awkwardness. I feel like I should buy the guy a drink, something. He did, after all, return my keys.

"Can I, um, buy you a drink for returning my keys?" A ghost of a smile starts at the corner of his lips, and great Valhalla, he's got a beautiful smile. What little glimpse of a smile he does offer me, reaches all the way to his eyes, and fuck me on a Friday, they're gorgeous. Long lashes, the slash of a manly brow, and the palest blue irises I've ever seen. They set the tone for his sun-kissed skin. It's almost as if they're glowing. *Why, Freya? Why must you do this to me?* Of course, my geekiness comes out in the form of internal blubbering. Get used to it. I can go on like this for hours. I take another long look. I never used to be a girl who went for a guy with hair longer than mine, but his long, dark locks are pulled back away from his face and in a bun. A freaking *man-bun,* and he has at least two days' growth on his face.

"What does that say about me, if I let you buy the drinks?" Does he really want me to answer that? *Open your mouth, Jada, let words come forth with sound.*

"I don't know. What does it say?" He full-on smiles now, and it's a megawatt smile, meant to drop panties. Hundreds of thousands of thongs, with and without lace. Cute little bows where the ass starts. Okay, I need to stop. Like now. How long have I been staring at his mouth? Did he notice? His eyes are laughing. Yeah, he knows. But I stand there anyway, waiting for his response.

"It says I'm no man if I let a beautiful woman buy me a drink."

*Holy shit, Batman! He called me beautiful.*

I'm in way over my head. Like for serious. I need to cut my losses, throw in the towel, and go back to my motel. I need to drive to Dallas tomorrow. Dali and Poe are sure to be driving my aunt and uncle nuts. *No, you need to saddle up and take him out for a spin.* No. No. And just…well, okay, maybe?

"Okay. Wait, you are buying the drinks?"

"First and only round on me. Then you can drive home, and I'll forever remember the beautiful goddess I met by way of Sulphur, Louisiana."

Sold!

To the lady on fire.

Now would be a bad time to quote anchorman and invite him to the party in my pants, but dammit, Gina, I'm down. *Who are you and what have you done with Jada Alexander?* Good question. No fucking clue really.

But I reach out my hand. "I'm Jada." His eyes spark momentarily with what I think may be recognition. My mind must be playing tricks on me because there is no way we know each other.

"Nicklaus."

*I'm in love.* I'm in love with Nicklaus the hottie. Someone save me now. Before I throw myself at him. Nicklaus's walk has major swag, like, off the charts swag. And why do I keep noticing? This isn't going to be a hook-up. No, it's a drink, a simple nightcap. As I make my way through the crowd, some of the locals are staring me down. I never leave with a man. I don't walk in with any either. Not since idiot van dickums.

"So," I stumble. "What shall we drink to?" Nicklaus looks down at me, like down. Did I forget to mention his height? Like he could be Thor's older, much hotter brother, Vidor, Asgardian God of the Hunt. *Yes, and hell yes.* Nicklaus definitely has some Norse blood running deep in those veins. Well, I don't actually know what Vidor looks like because there are so many different variations of him, but if I had to describe him, it would be Nicklaus.

"Let's have a drink to chance meetings." Nicklaus signals a waitress, who all but eye fucks him as she takes our orders, and okay, I get it, he's hot. But I called dibs the moment he sat with me at the table. Our drinks arrive quickly, like the waitress, I think her name is Sandy, has been dying to get us, or should I say Nicklaus, a cold one.

"To chance meetings," I toast.

"To chance meetings." He watches me the entire time, and I can't put my finger on it, but it's like he's looking at me as if we've met before. There is an undeniable attraction between us; at least I hope there is. It could be all one-sided, but who really cares at this point? *It's just a drink, Jada, slow your roll.*

"So, Jada, you come here often?" I can't help it. My smile is a mile wide because it's the cheesiest line ever, but I actually think he's serious.

"Why, Klaus, you wound me with your pick-up line. I thought for sure you were better than that."

He's still staring at me, and now the look on his face is incredulous. Like no one, and I mean no one can call him Klaus but those nearest and dearest to him.

"Can you say that again?" he asks. This time, his voice is soft, barely above a whisper, and if I hadn't already been all up in his beautiful face watching his lips move and his throat work, I may not have heard him.

"What would you like me to say? The entire sentence again, or just your name?"

"My name."

"Klaus." I say it slowly, hold the 's' a little longer than necessary, and watch, fascinated, as he closes his eyes and dare I say…groans. This guy is too good to be true. It's like someone up above in the heavens knows this is the kind of man I'd take my clothes off for. Now, I don't normally say what I'm about to say next, but I'm young, I'm safe, and well, if this guy is a serial killer, I know several ways to disarm a man. But I'm feeling the buzz and I'm totally feeling *him*. So, what the hell. Here goes nothing.

"Why don't we finish our drinks and head back to my place."

"My place" is a motel room that I'm only staying in for one night, and I've never had a one-night stand before. And I have to admit, I've bashed plenty of my college friends for indulging. But here I am, about to go for the gusto. *Full speed ahead, Steam Boat Willy style.* Only, I'm not a mouse, and I can't whistle for shit.

"You want me to come back to your place?" he asks, and I swear his accent is melting my panties. If I weren't made of sturdier stock, I'd be a pile of goo right here in my goddamn chair. By the moon of the goddess, I'm one horny girl. *Don't get nervous, Jada,* I'm coaching myself now because I'm a nervous wreck. I kid you not, at this very moment, I'm comparing him to every comic book superhero I ever wanted to bone me; and for some reason, Thor's older brother is forefront in my mind. Again. Aaaaah, the God of the Hunt. *Vidor, you lucky bastard, you're about to get laid.*

I want to laugh out loud because, yeah, that shit is funny. Maybe not to anyone else who had the pleasure to—or maybe not so pleasurable—walk through my warped mind, but who cares. I'm taking this Viking god home with me tonight, and I plan on doing all sorts of dirty things. I mean, things that shouldn't be done to a man but every man wants done to him. Or, I could totally flip the script and let him have his wicked way with me.

No!

I gotta play it safe, be demure and not too pushy. Men don't like pushy women. Shit! I already asked him to my room. That right there is more than forward, it's a direct line to, 'if you ask a guy to your room on first contact, you're probably a whore.'

"Never mind, I don't know what I'm saying." I try and recant.

But Nicklaus is having none of that. He has a determined look on his face, and it's the kind of look that says he's a bit hesitant. Like *I'm* the serial killer, but he's intrigued enough to give it a go anyway.

SCORE!

"No, it's fine, I'll follow you."

"Sure." Not gonna turn down the opportunity for a hot fling with a Viking god. I'd be crazy. All the gods and goddesses above sitting high and pretty in their kingdoms will surely curse me if I don't take advantage of the male across from me.

I grab my keys, slap some money on the table, and remind Nicklaus that it's the tip since he offered to buy the drinks. We make it outside, and my phone starts going off. Ugh, Caroline. She always has a way of texting or calling at the most inopportune times. Once, she texted while I was in the middle of my S.E.E.K. final, and that was just the other day. Needless to say, my commanding officer didn't like that at all. Not one bit. I got a ten-point drop for not putting my phone on silent, and I know he went easy on me because he'd once failed a guy for answering a text message.

I jump in my car, turn it on, check my mirror, and see he's on a bike. Not some little Ninja Kawasaki either, he's on a straight-up man's bike. I'm talking a Dyna Low Rider, 103 twin cam engine. And…now you've spotted the gearhead in me. Not only do I dig comic books, I also have a lady boner for bikes. Klaus flashes his lights at me, and that's my signal to get a move on. It's time to do the damn thing and do it well.

The motel isn't far. It's down the street, around the corner, and half a mile up the road. There is no pretense; the moment I hit the door, the hard wall of his body is caging me in as I go for my key card. He's mumbling something in his native tongue; and fuck, it's a language I do not speak—and I speak six. But not this one. It does nothing but spur me on to find the key card that has been swallowed by my not-so-ginormous purse. It's like he's saying a prayer, and I want to say one, too because I can feel the hard, and I mean rock-hard, length of his cock against my back.

*That's all mine,* I think. *All mine.*

Oh my, I'm one lucky girl.

"Got it!" I say, excited that I finally found the keycard. His fingers are in my hair, which is up in a ponytail. I didn't have time to condition it this morning so it's thick and a little dry, but an easy fix once I get out of the shower. But first, a little one-night-stand-a-la-hottie. The door pushes open, and before I even have a chance to get a grasp on what's about to happen, Nicklaus has me turned in his arms and latches on to my mouth. Quite magnificently, too. His lips are warm and soft, and his tongue tastes like his drink mixed with mine, and that is not a bad thing. I moan into the kiss and give just as good as he does, but I'm hoping it's better. Because kissing is one of my things. I may be a nerd, but I'm a great kisser. I could give you a list of references, but I'd rather just think about what's going on right now.

His hands move to my waist, and they're hot against my skin. Except for the cool metal on his ring finger, on his left hand. What. The. Fuck. No, no, that's not right. I decide it's a trick of my mind, but I feel the ring again as he roams my ribcage, and this time, I can't mistake it. There's a fucking band on his ring finger, of his left hand. *Whathewhat*! No, no, fuck, no! This isn't happening!

I pull back, panting, and grab his left hand, bringing it up to my face. I'm eyeing him, then I'm eyeing the ring. I'm pissed off because Nicklaus is an excellent kisser, he had me revved and ready to discard all my clothes, skipping over the foreplay and heading straight for ecstasy. I was willing, primed, but the man standing in front of me is fucking *married*. Married! How I wish Long Duck Dong were here to clarify that this is not really true and instead just a language barrier, and that my Jake—who is actually Nicklaus—is in fact not married. And, somehow, someway, Molly Ringwald—although I'm way taller, and darker of skin, though I have a flawless pair of lips just like her—is in fact inside the church, trying to grab my bitch of a sister's train. And Nicklaus is waiting for me, not in his cherry-red Corvette, but on his Dyna Low Rider, helmet-head and all. Wait, Long Duck Dong said *I'd* be the married one. Only I'm not. He is. Fuckity fuck, fuck!

"You kissed me on the mouth!" I screech.

He takes a step back and looks at me like I've lost my mind.

"I let you, a married man, kiss me on the mouth," I say again. "The fuck is wrong with you?" I yell, pointing towards the door. "Out. Get out, right now!"

I normally get flustered during confrontations. But I'm hyped on alcohol. I know it because I can still feel the slight buzz, which is now a whaling roar inside my skull.

"Jada, please, let me explain." He's pleading, and he looks so remorseful, but I can't be bothered with that. Oh, hell no, I'm not going to listen to the excuses of a married man. No way, no how. NO. CAN. DO.

"Klaus, you need to leave, or I'll make you leave, and you won't like how that goes down." I go to stand in front of my nightstand because if he doesn't move, I'm creating my first official Internal Affairs investigation 'cause I'm going to grab my gun and pump two into his body. One in his hand, and the other in the appendage I was just about to let pound into me.

Damn it.

I really wanted him to work out all my kinks.

"If you'll let me explain…"

"Nope." I shake my head dramatically and go for my gun in the drawer."

He must know what's about to happen because his eyes get wide, and he starts to back up towards the door. "I'm sorry, Jada, truly sorry."

"Yeah, you better be sorry. Now get the fuck out."

He opens the door, and the sound of it clicking shut after he leaves deflates me. I'm done. So mad and hurt. I was really hoping he was going to be a good guy. Someone I could really get into, even if just for one night. He's just like my ex-boyfriend. *Fake ass motherfuckers.* That's what men are.

2

THREE YEARS LATER

"Agent Alexander?" I hear my name being called and sigh. I really don't have time for this. Dali is in top form, and every time an officer or one of the firemen comes over, I lose sight of my dog. It doesn't make me feel any better. Dali's not on a leash, but I don't want her wandering too far, I know it's her job, I get it. But if my dog gets hurt, I'm going to lose my mind. *Up in here. Up in here.* Gah. I geek out at the worst possible times, but who can blame me. The guys over at fire department do a brilliant job getting everyone out. Truth be told, I crushed on the guys that responded to the initial call for about five seconds. Then, I was all business. There are no casualties; only a few victims suffering from smoke inhalation. And one lady lost her purse in the fire. I was called in; rather, Dali was called in, because this was no accident. My girl's won a shit-ton of medals since we've been on the job, and there's talk about sending us overseas to help our brothers and sisters in arms over in the desert.

Dali and I had this conversation already, and Poe even backed us up when we said, "Hell, no!" It's not that I don't love my country, I do. But sending Dali and me thousands of miles away from Poe, my black cat, is a straight-up deal breaker. Some people think I'm weird because of my love for my animals. But at the end of the day, humans are out, and fur babies are in.

"Yes?" I turn to see one of the men from the fire department. looking over at me. It's Ken Forrest—brown eyes, black hair, and he screams ex-military. Did I forget to mention he's oh so sexy? And he's coming my way. I can see the end of Dali's tail as she searches through what's left of the building.

"You keep showing up at our sites, I'm gonna start thinking you're stalking me, little lady." This comes from one of the other men who responded to the call. I can't remember his name.

"In your dreams. I'm way too much woman for you to handle. Besides, Dali and Poe wouldn't give you their seal of approval," I joke back.

It's true, too, and the weirdest thing. I tried bringing guys home, maybe once or twice since I got to Dallas, and each time, my fur babies went bonkers. It's like some huge cosmic joke from the god of animals that I'm not to have the pleasure of a man. Not unless I take my pleasure outside my home. Because trust me, this girl is on the prowl. Okay, not really, I don't trust men. I've had my share of epic fuckups and don't need a repeat. Now…I'm *all* about the hookup. Well, if you count my five-date rule, then an additional two dates to get to third base. Unfortunately, they usually don't stick around that long, but I digress. Kenneth is talking to me, and I need to pay attention.

"We have the chili cook-off this weekend, you should come by the station and bring your best chili."

"Yeah, that sounds like something I can get into. Can Dali come?"

"Yeah, it's no problem at all. The kids will love her, and Skye is making some kickass pastries."

"Pastries?" I ask, about to make fun of him because big, tall Ken just used the word "pastries" in the same sentence as kickass. How does he still make it look cool? He's got black soot all over his brow and cheek, and his suit reeks of smoke, yet he still manages to pull off major swag. Too bad I look at him like an older brother. All the guys I've met so far while on the job are like older brothers, and they all keep trying to get me to come down to the damn station.

"Bring your appetite, kid."

"We done here? I have to finish checking the building out."

"Yeah, you find anything, let the captain know, there's been a series of fires like this in and around the city lately, and we can't put our finger on it."

"Agent Alexander at your service." I salute him and walk off. It's good the Dallas unit. and the ATF are collaborating because Ken isn't wrong. This isn't a series of coincidences; it's something more. Even Dali knows it; she hasn't stopped sniffing around, but if there is something here, my baby girl will find it.

---

I have music playing as I make sure my chili is nice and spicy. The boys at the station can eat a person out of house and home. I grab my Carolina Cooker cast iron crockpot and grin. It looks like a witch's cauldron and holds more than ten pounds of chili. It's heavy as hell, and I am lucky my ranch hand, Thomas, is there to help me load it in the truck.

"Thanks, Thomas."

"No problem, Jada." He gives me a quick grin before he runs back into his yard. He left his front window open, and I can hear the game on in the living room. Boys and their sports. I'll never get used to it. I'm only about a half hour outside of Dallas in Van Alstyne. I stay in what equates to a farm on more than two hundred acres of land off a small lake, complete with trees, a creek, many ponds, and a view to die for. I scrimped and saved until I was able to afford the house and got it on a steal. I don't have any animals on my farm that I lovingly call Alexander Hills—outside of Dali and Poe, of course—but I plan to very soon. Right now, it's just the fur babies and me. Thomas stays in the cottage house that sits adjacent to my garage, and he's been more than helpful when it comes to the ins and outs of keeping the place running.

Dali is in the front seat, strapped into her doggy seat belt because let's face it, dogs and chili don't get along. Not even on the coldest of days.

"All right, girl, you're going to play with the kids while Momma eats some chili and chops it up with the local firemen. If I so happen to find a man, promise you'll behave?" I say to Dali. Her head is currently out the window, taking in the air, but it's like she can hear me and actually understands what I'm talking about because she pulls her head in, looks at me, and I swear she gives me an exaggerated eye roll.

"Aah, come on, Dali girl. Momma needs to have a good time. I'm not talking about forever. I'm just talking about right now."

Nothing.

My dog is ignoring me.

If Poe were here, he'd probably do the same thing. Those two are an unlikely but loveable pair. There is something about today; I don't know what it is. And I kid you not, I have butterflies in my stomach; like today could be the day I run into Mr. Right Now. As I make the left-hand turn into the station and see the cars all parked in a row, my eyes don't miss the Dyna sitting in the driveway.

Oh, my wheezy, grapes, and peanuts! A Dyna.

Motorcycles are my thing.

Like.

My.

Thang.

Go on, throw the southern twang on the end there. You can do it. Now say it with me. *"Motorcycles are my thang."*

But I'm not gonna lie, the other thought ghosting

through my mind is Klaus von married man. That was one guy that left a lasting impression. Not only on me but my mind, my body; hell, he'd even shown up in my dreams a few times. And seeing the Dyna just brings it all back.

I park the car, right next to the two-wheel hottie, and pray to the gearhead gods that the body attached to the seat of that hotrod belongs to a warrior. A warrior of old, a warrior of new, hell, give me Karl Urban in *Pathfinder*, and I'm your gal. Because only a beast of a man would roll up on a Dyna, and all the men of Dallas Fire and Rescue are beasts. *Rawr.*

I open the car door just as Kenneth steps out into the hot Texas sun. He's on his phone chatting with someone, and when he sees me, he gives me a chin lift. I reciprocate and walk around to the passenger side to let Dali out. She won't leave my side until I give her the all clear. But I can tell she sees someone she wants to say hi to. Her tail is wagging frantically, and if she could jump up and down and scream, "Mommy, can I?" repeatedly, she would.

I walk to the back of my car and open the trunk, about to yell out to Kenneth for some much-needed assistance, when a blast, no, a *chill* from my past skates right up the back of my spine and into my ear.

"Can I help you with that?" The smooth,

caramelized sound of his voice could melt ice on the coldest of days.

Holy fuck on a fried cheese stick. It's Nicklaus.

I want to turn around and scream the house down. Ever since that night three years ago, I've had nothing but bad luck when it comes to men. I've compared them all to the one intense kiss Klaus and I shared back in my motel room, and dammit, I'm ruined…completely ruined. There is a small voice in the back of my mind that says, *fuck it,* throw caution to the wind and jump his bones already. But I can't. He's married. Fucking married.

I won't ever be that girl.

Nope.

Not.

Me.

Ever.

His arms reach out and enclose me as he reaches for the pot of chili, and I know he does it on purpose. *Freaking douche nozzle.* He's trying to get me riled up. *Or does he even know it's me*? I wonder.

"It's good to see you again, Jada." *Well, that answers that question.* His body is so close that I can feel the heat of his words. Dali, the traitor, is sitting there, tail wagging, big eyes hopeful. What does she expect? I can't. He's married.

"Klaus, baby," a female voice says over the roar in my head. "Baby, who's your friend?"

Great. His wife. I don't want to turn around and look. I can't. My limbs are locked in place, and a quiet rage takes over as I think of that night back in my room. He followed me home with every intention of cheating on his wife.

"Tammy, this is a good friend of mine, Jada. I met her three years ago in Sulphur, Louisiana."

*You did a hell of a lot more than* meet me.

I'm seething, and right when I'm about to turn around, his arm goes around my waist, and he turns me to him.

"What the hell?" I say.

At the same time, Tammy, who I can't see because Klaus's big-ass broad shoulders are blocking my view says, "What in the world is going on here?"

I try with Herculean effort to get out of his arms, but he squeezes me tighter and says against my forehead—yes, my forehead, "You are not getting away this time, gorgeous."

"Who you calling gorgeous?"

"You," he says as he steps back and releases me somewhat. Dali nudges me forward, and I almost fall back into his arms.

"Dali, calm down."

What the hell is she doing? Dali never, and I mean *never* acts this way with men. Especially men I'm attracted to. Apparently, if they've already put a ring on someone else's finger, they are fair game to my traitorous dog.

"She's all right. She knows good people when she sees them."

I grunt.

"Tammy, Jada," he says to the woman, who I can now see clearly. She's tall, svelte, not an ounce of fat on her, and she's decked out in denim cut-offs, a Harley tank top, and cowboy boots. Damn, I can't fault his wife one bit. She's definitely a looker. If I swung both ways, I'd invite her into my bed. What? Don't act like you haven't checked out a pretty woman before. We all have, we're all offenders. There's no hate here. I know beautiful when I see it, and she's it. I totally feel like Boof in *Teen Wolf* because, let's face it, Nicklaus is a wolf, and I'm the friend with the unreciprocated crush.

My mind starts to wander into movie land, and I do a mass comparison of all the situations I could relate to at this very moment. Like when Molly Ringwald is being sized up by Seth's douchebag girlfriend in *Pretty in Pink*, even though she's the one being all whorish. Or when Taylor pours her drink down Laney's dress on purpose. Yup, that would be me, only I can't say anything bad about his wife because she's like awesomely beautiful. Freakishly, if you really want my opinion, and everything on her is natural, from the size of her perky breasts, right down to her toned stomach and long-ass legs.

My brain hasn't caught up to what's happening around me because now Kenneth is standing there with a strange look on his face.

"You okay, Jada?"

"Huh?"

"I asked if you were all right?"

"Yeah, yeah, I'm good. Just got caught up in the moment."

"You're having a moment with our mechanic, Klaus?" Kenneth asks, confused.

"Yeah, and um, his wife, Tammy."

"Wife?" Nicklaus and Kenneth say at the same time.

Kenneth looks between the three of us, and now I'm the one truly confused. I hate when I check out, it only happens when I'm really uncomfortable, or when I'm overly excited. I'm totally screwed. I know it.

Tammy doesn't correct me, so I'm not sure why both men are stuck on stupid.

"She's not my wife."

"I thought Tammy was with your friend, Hector?" Kenneth asks.

"Yeah, she is, but Jada here thinks I'm married."

I turn in his arms then and look up—way up—into his eyes. They're lighter than I remember, arctic, but not cold, just fathomless.

"You're not married?" I ask. I'm praying again to the gods of old and new, because if dude is not attached, I swear to all that is holy, I'm dropping off the chili and taking him home. *Whoa. Slow your roll. Slow your roll. You are not taking him home.* Right.

Be calm.

Play it cool.

He could be with someone.

*Please don't be attached. Pretty please.* Someone give me a break. Just this once, I want to get what I want.

"No, and if you'd let me explain the last time we met, you would have known that."

"I would have?" I whisper.

"Yeah, gorgeous, you would have."

There he goes with the name again. Why is he calling me that?

"Well, if you two are done with the reunion, I'd like to eat some chili. Tammy, call Hector out here to help with the pot. You two, take your time getting reacquainted," Kenneth says. But neither of us are listening. We're both staring at one another, and it's already hotter than black asphalt in California.

---

Klaus is the mechanic for Dallas Fire and Rescue. He's like the head mechanic, and everyone here loves him. How I'd never run into him until now is a mystery.

"You look really nice, Jada."

I look like my normal self. I'm in a pair of boyfriend jeans and a Suicide Squad shirt. My hair is shorter. I cut it about six months ago.

Geez. The way he says my name incinerates me. I want to be mad at him, but I can't be. He's not freaking married. At least, not now he isn't. But he was wearing a wedding band during our last encounter.

"I need you to explain to me how you were not married the first time we met, when you clearly had on a wedding band. Don't tell me you were separated, because that would mean you were still married," I say sternly with a tilt of my head and an arch of my brow.

His piercing blue gaze is haunting for a minute. Clearly, there is a story, but it doesn't look like he's willing to get into it right this minute.

"Can we wait until after. I'd like to talk to you alone, when everyone isn't around."

Can I wait?

Do I even *want* to wait?

*Just hear him out, Jada*, my mind admonishes.

"Fine. Whatever you want to talk about can wait until after. But I do expect us to talk."

"We will." Nicklaus grabs my hand and leads me over to the others, where they all sit and chat around a table. Dali is following closely behind. The guys at the station all love her, and she seems to like them, as long as none of them get fresh with me. Dali's definition of *fresh* is anyone who gives me a hug. So when the captain walks over to me and pulls me in for a quick squeeze, Dali is there, voicing her opinion rather excitedly.

"Calm down, Dali girl. It's just the captain, and he's so not my type."

"You act like the dog understands you." This comes from Tammy, the hottie in the biker gear.

"Oh, she does. She was one of the smartest dogs in the S.E.E.K. program. Without her, there would be no ATF career for me. I'm basically just her handler. She does all the work."

"How did the two of you become a team?" Another woman I'm not familiar with says this, but if she was invited for chili, chances are she's good people.

"Dali and I go way back. She basically saved my life. I was harassed by a group of drunk college students when I was in school myself. Out late, partying it up…you know, wrong place, wrong time. Well, they cornered me, and there she was. She was a little thing at the time, but you'd never know it by her heroic barking. She was loud enough that a passerby heard her and came to find out what all the ruckus was. Turned out, he was campus police."

"Wow."

Nicklaus, who still has a hold of my hand, squeezes me gently. It isn't much, but the idea that he cares is certainly conveyed by that one action. I swear I'm not a girly girl. I'm all about rubbing dirt on my aches and salt in my wounds, but that small gesture from him means so much in that moment, I think I get a little teary-eyed.

He lets go of my hand to pull me into his side, and against my ear, he whispers, "Dali is my new best friend."

I can't say anything. My heart is beating entirely too fast due to our intimate moment. We haven't even had the 'talk' yet. But somehow, the two of us together just makes sense. No one at the station says a word about the exchange or his PDA with me. It's like we've been a couple for years. We eat, we drink beer, we talk. Dali stays with us the entire time. Nicklaus even pulls me into his lap as he talks shop with some of the guys. And what do I do? I soak that shit up, enjoying every minute of it.

## 3

I don't want to leave the station. I am afraid the night with Nicklaus is over, but he quickly puts my mind to rest when he walks me over to my car and asks to follow me home. I can't say no. How can I? I want to hear him out, and maybe pick up where we left off three years ago. I turn a thirty-minute drive into a fifteen-minute one. The lights at Thomas's place are out, but my front porch light is on. The sun has just started to go down, so it isn't that late.

Klaus parks his bike behind my car and is at my door, helping me to get out. He even walks around and unbuckles Dali from her seat in the front. Again, she seems to be really enamored with him, and I can't fault her. He is definitely someone people want to be around.

"You go unlock the door, Jada, I'll go grab your pot out of the back."

"Okay," I whisper, sounding like some helpless female twit from one of those girly shows. Me, Jada Alexander, independent woman extraordinaire, is playing the helpless female. I stealthily unlock my front door, trying my best not to disturb Poe. My cat has an uncanny way of greeting strangers. Especially men. He will literally hiss and spray. Yes, hiss and spray. Like he's marking his territory, telling any male who dares to come within one inch of me to back off.

But this time when I open the door, there is no black male cat to greet me. It's as if the house is empty. Dali saunters past me and goes straight for her food bowl. I set my keys on the counter and thank the mighty cleaning gods that I actually cleaned my house. Klaus walks in and takes in all that is my farmhouse. I pray he likes it. Most people don't get me. Okay, correction, nobody gets me. I'm not your average bear. Like seriously, my house is the exact opposite of what a farmhouse should look like.

I know what you're thinking. Exactly what is a farmhouse supposed to look like, right? Well, the décor should be country and welcoming. But I have a replica of Bumblebee in the entrance to my house. Not the exact specifications, of course, but damn near close. Klaus takes it in and whistles low under his breath.

"Well, that's not something you see every day."

I laugh it off with a somewhat un-lady-like snort. If the man can't get down with Bumblebee, then he doesn't need to be here. *Wrong.* Warning bells go off in my head as I play back the better part of our make-out session from what seems like forever ago. The man can kiss. He is made for kissing, and if memory serves, and boy does it ever, I was two seconds away from having my way with him until that nasty ring reared its ugly head. He said we'd talk about it, and now is as good a time as any. This can't go any further until I hear his explanation.

"You said we'd talk about the ring."

"I did, didn't I," he says, thoughtfully. "Where would you like to talk?"

My brain screams bedroom, floor, shower, couch, in front of the couch, outside on the back deck, anywhere this man wants to go that leads to us being horizontal, I am okay with. My body is all too on board with that plan. But I rein in my inner temptress. I could say *slut*, but who am I kidding. I don't get down like that. Never have and never will. Klaus gets this heated look in his eyes before rubbing his hand down his face.

"Don't stare at me like that. I really want to talk. When you look at me like you want to consume me, all the blood rushes from my head to my cock."

The nerves in my stomach are now all aflutter with lust.

I look down.

Yep, blood is swinging south all right, and *dude,* I'm so not ready for this.

"Let's go into the kitchen. I'll make us some coffee and serve up some pie. How does that sound?"

"Conducive to a conversation that I hope you're able to take in."

Why would he hope?

This can't be good. I'm about to panic, but Klaus places a hand on my waist and turns me toward him.

"Everything is going to be all right, Jada. I know it."

He kisses the tip of my nose, and I almost melt. From a kiss…on the nose. *Whoa.* On shaky legs, I make my way over to the kitchen. Which, by the way, is decked out in DC gear. I was originally going to go with the whole *Nightmare before Christmas* theme, but my guest bathroom downstairs already boasts some spiffy Skellington gear. I'm surprised he doesn't mention my decorative style or criticize me. He just seems to be taking it all in.

I put on coffee and set the apple pie out on the counter. Klaus is eyeing my kitchen with a smile on his face. When the coffee is served, and the apple pie is piled high on our plates, I sit across from him at the table. He doesn't say much at first. Just stares. His beautiful gaze roams over my face, and although I don't know what he's thinking, my body is hearing whatever telepathic commands he's throwing out. I watch as his eyes drop to my lips, then move up again to my eyes.

"I really want to kiss you right now," he says, his voice deep and heavily accented. Still there, and still just as sexy as the first time I heard him speak.

"Well, I would agree with you, but you said we should talk, and as much as I want to be kissed by you, I need to know what the deal is with your marriage and why you didn't tell me the first time we met."

Klaus clears his throat.

"My wife and son died almost five years ago," he says slowly. His eyes are filled with true pain. He's reliving the exact moment he lost them. The agony, clear on his face, pierces me deeply. I want to say something but don't get the chance because he keeps talking. "It took me a while to get over the fact that they were gone. I was in the car with them when it happened. I survived. They didn't. Went through a year of rehab. Had to learn to walk again. Severe spinal damage. They thought for sure I'd be in a wheelchair for the rest of my life."

"I'm so, so sorry," I whisper as tears clog my throat.

"It wasn't your fault. I know most people think the appropriate response to that is 'sorry.' But no one can be sorry. Only me. I'm the one who's sorry." Klaus clears his throat. I know his words are stuck. I can tell he's deeply affected.

How am I supposed to even respond to that? The whole "I'm sorry" is an automatic response to someone's pain. Most people would have accepted the apology, but not Klaus.

"I don't know what it feels like to lose someone you love, but I've seen a lot of death in the last couple of years. I've talked to families and watched as their whole world was turned upside down. All I can do is offer my condolences."

Klaus nods his head before continuing on.

"Anyway, the night we met, I was passing through. Stopping off to visit my wife's parents. She was from Sulphur." His gaze catches mine as a pit opens up in my stomach. Sulphur isn't big, but it isn't small either. Everyone pretty much knows everyone, which is why I want to throw up now. He's talking about Amelia. Amelia Ingels. My and Caroline's best friend, Amelia. We'd grown up together, said we'd get married and have babies all at the same time, and live on the same street. I hadn't been able to make the funeral. My flight was delayed. I'd sat inside of JFK, bawling my eyes out at the injustice of it all. And her son, little Nico. I'd seen pictures of her beautiful boy. Why couldn't I remember ever seeing Nicklaus?

"You knew my wife. She talked about you all the time."

This was wrong.

On so many levels, wrong.

Like junior high and high school wrong, when girls swapped boyfriends, and they'd all be in the same social circle, wrong. I can't do this. I can't get bone, or hell, even think about be boned, by my dead best friend's widowed husband. No. No. And hell no!

I put a spoonful of pie in my mouth to try and combat the dread in the pit of my stomach. I look over at Klaus. He's watching me closely. Waiting to see my reaction, I'm sure. But what the hell can I say to him? "Sorry you lost your wife and son, but you gotta go. Get to stepping. Kick rocks, dirt, gravel, whatever the hell my road is paved with." *Like that will work.* I could tell him to take his sexy ass off my property and never darken my doorstep again. But what kind of person would I be? Obviously, he doesn't understand the severity of this situation.

"Um." I clear my throat and try again. "Um, Klaus. I don't know what to say."

"Don't say anything. I can tell by the look in your eyes. You're shocked, but Amelia told me all about you. And before she left me, she wanted me to find you, seek you out."

"What? Why?"

"Because she said the only other woman who would be as good to me as she was would be you."

Mic drop.

He did not just drop that bomb at my fucking feet.

Holy hell on a wet Sunday. How does one even respond to something like that?

---

My tongue is glued to the roof of my mouth because I don't know what to fucking say to that. Amelia was always a bit wacky, but this, she went way too far with this shit.

"Look, Klaus, I don't know what Amelia may or may not have said about me, but I can assure you, she was joking. Seriously, Amelia would never want me for you. Not in a million years."

His face contorts with what looks like anger. Why is he mad at me? I'm not the one trying to hook up with my dead wife's best friend.

"You're wrong. She may have been dying when she said it, but that doesn't change the fact that she did. I didn't plan to seek you out. Hell, it took me an entire year to even work up the courage to go to Sulphur, and even then, I didn't plan to run into you. But I did, and, well, things changed."

"Dude, we haven't seen each other in three years."

"So?"

"So! So?! Are you out of your mind? We can't hook up. Not now. Not ever. Friends. That, I'll agree to, but hooking up? No. And as much as it pains me to say it,"—I shake my head furiously—"heck no."

His eyes darken to a deeper shade of blue. Just moments ago, they were light. Damn blue-eyed hottie.

"You say you just want to be friends, yes?"

"Yes." I nod vehemently.

Nicklaus chuckles to himself before straightening his face.

"Friends it is then, Jada Alexander."

"Friends it is."

Nicklaus stands and rounds the table and pulls me in for what can only be called an awkward hug. He doesn't say another word as he heads out my front door. Not one single word. But I have this funny feeling that the topic of our friendship, or non-romantic relationship, is not off the table. My Spidey-senses are tingling. I can't put my finger on it, but some major shit is about to go down.

4

My alarm goes off to the tune of Kid Cudi's, *Immortal*. It's Sunday, or is it Saturday? I don't remember which. I stayed up late, like super late, thinking about all Klaus had said. I need to talk to Caroline, but sometimes, she just doesn't understand. I can hear her saying, "Well, if Amelia said it was okay, bang him like you need him every day of the week." Yeah, that pretty much sums up my very relaxed and open friend.

Dali is at the foot of the bed, and Poe is sitting in the chair next to the window. His bright green eyes tell me I should have been up at least an hour ago to feed him. Dali, as always, is happy to sleep in. My fur babies have separate schedules, and their own set of rules they expect me to adhere to. *Gotta love the kids.*

"All right, Poe, what's it gonna be, chicken or beef?" I ask.

*Meow.*

"Chicken it is, then."

That's what he said. Chicken. Meow meant chicken. If I got a purr, that would be beef. I know my children. I pull myself out of bed and make my way into the kitchen. Poe is following close behind and not like your normal cat would. I had ledges installed in the house. Some of them are high, others are low. There are even tunnels linking the rooms together, and before you knock it and call me crazy, don't. Cats are natural predators. They need to feel like they're stalking their food, or spying on their would-be human masters. I wasn't about to let my cat feel like he was totally domesticated. So I had the house cat-pimped Poe follows me on one of the higher ledges, the pitter-patter of his feet is almost silent. He hasn't quite mastered his stealth yet, but I'm not giving up hope.

When I reach the pantry and grab the chicken, I turn to find Poe waiting for me on top of the island. *Okay, maybe he's moved it up a notch in his stealth tactics.* Before I can even open the can of cat food, there is a knock on my door. Thomas is off on Sundays, so who could that be?

"Be right back, gotta go see who's at the door," I tell my cat.

When I reach the entry, I look through the peephole, and who is it? Why, it's the bane of my sexual frustration. Yes, frustrated, because I got off not once but twice last night with just my hand. That's like never happened before. I usually need my B.O.B. for that kind of work, but, oh, hell no. A good imagination will take you a long way, and I have one hell of an imagination. I look down. I know my hair is a mess, and I'm wearing bikini panties and a Pac-man tee shirt. *Fuck a duck.*

Yanking open my front door, I glare at Klaus.

"What are you doing here?" I ask angrily.

He eyes me from head to toe. The movement is slow, sensual, and makes heat rise in my cheeks. Dear God in heaven, but why is this man looking at me like this? It's too early for this, but I suddenly realize why he's staring so hard. *Shit. Shit. Shit.* Did someone order dork a la range? Because, seriously, life can't get any crazier than it already is. I'm practically naked. I knew what I was wearing, and instead of putting on clothes before I answered, I flung the door wide open like a crazy person. *You should have put clothes on.* I should have, but I didn't. What does that say about me? *That you're deliberately trying to bait and hook you a man.* If I had the remote control from *Click*, I'd seriously be redoing this moment. Played it better. More level-headed. But it's too late for that now.

"Good morning to you to, *friend,*" Klaus says with laughter in his eyes. He doesn't even ask permission to come in, he just shoulders past me, and he's holding coffee. From effin Raldi's. And why the fuck do I even care? How does he even know I'd kill a bitch for Raldi's coffee? Then I remember. Fucking Kenneth. He's the only one who knows about my secret love of Raldi's. He must have put Klaus up on his game. *Traitor. Now you're trying to help a brother out by giving him the deets on me. Oh, we'll just have to see about that.*

"You can't be here. It's early, like way early."

Klaus looks over at me from the living room and shrugs.

"Put some clothes on, *friend,* unless when you said we could be friends, you meant some other kind of friend. Like the kind with benefits."

His voice, it does it for me every time, and how freaking sick is that?

*Put a lid on it, Alexander, that's Amelia's man.*

Right.

Dead best friend's husband. I have to remember that.

I stomp into my room, grab a pair of sweats, and scratch Dali's belly.

"Come on, girl, if I have to get up, so do you. Besides, there's a man in the house."

At that, Dali's ears perk up. See, I knew my dog had my back. Poe would jump on board too, especially since Klaus interrupted his breakfast. I make my way to the front of the house and I can hear Klaus's deep, accented voice rumbling through my kitchen. What's he doing in my kitchen? When I round the corner, I stop dead in my tracks. Klaus is feeding my cat.

Let me repeat that.

*Klaus is feeding my cat.*

As in Poe.

*Poe.*

Who doesn't like anyone, like anyone at all. Especially another male.

What planet am I on? And why is my cat loving the hell out of Mr. Intruder?

I clear my throat, and Klaus turns around with a smug grin on his face. *Oh, how I want to wipe that grin off your face with my lips.* What!? No!

"You're getting pretty cozy there with my cat, Klaus," I say, crossing my arms. His eyes go dark for a moment as he zeroes in on my chest.

"Pussies love me, what can I say?" There's that devil of a smile again. He's teasing me, and I'm doing my best not to fall for it.

"I want to take you somewhere."

"What?"

"Do you speak English? I know my accent is there, but it's not that bad is it?"

"Last time I checked, *friends* don't just show up at,"—I look over at the kitchen wall clock—"seven in the morning and expect to be greeted with a smile. Right now, you're my foe, definitely not welcomed."

To that, he laughs. It's deep and rolls as it washes over me, infusing me with a warmth that feels amazing. I'm in so much trouble with this guy. *Amelia, my love. When I die, you better meet me at the pearly gates. I'm gonna punch you, like right in the kisser.* In my sick, twisted mind, I can so see my friend laughing her ass off about my current predicament.

"Jada, drink your coffee and go and put some actual clothes on. I'll finish up here with Poe and Dali."

"How do you know my animals' names?"

He winks at me.

Winks!

Then, he's on the move, stalking towards me. His gait is smooth, and dude has swag, loads of it. He walks like he has nothing to worry about, nothing to fear. I hadn't realized just how attractive his walk was until now. Was he this confident the first time we met? I try and think back, but my brain short circuits because Klaus is all up in my personal space.

"What I say, Jada?"

My mind clouds with lust, large clouds of the potent stuff permeate my brain. *Now is not the time for this. Focus, girl. Focus.*

"Um, you said I needed to drink my coffee and get dressed."

"Right. Now, you gonna do that for me, or are you going to make things harder on yourself."

What did he say? Did he say he was going to go hard himself? *Whatthewhat?*

Ugh.

He's too close. His exhales are mingling with mine, and my breath can't be all that great at this particular moment in time. Somehow, I manage to step back, but he steps forward. I want to cover my mouth with my hand, but that would be too obvious, so I stop breathing altogether. My eyes are wide, and my heart is beating to the tune of *I wanna Rock* by Twisted Sister. Yup, I'm a hot ass mess.

"I want you to get hard," I whisper, then gasp loudly as I realize what words just came out of my mouth.

"I am, baby."

Oh, double stuff Oreo cookies and ice-cold milk. He called me "baby." *Swoon.*

And, yeah, embarrassing moment number gazillion, I sway, actually *sway* when he calls me baby.

His hand goes to my waist, where he holds me steady. Fuck that. I'm not gonna fall for his crap. No and no. I close my eyes briefly, take a deep breath, and move his hand from my waist, then slide past him while grabbing my cup of coffee.

"I'll get dressed, but only because you have no business seeing me in my jammies. And I'm not saying thank you for the coffee. It's owed to me because you're here way too early. Whatever you have planned for today better not be about trying to get into my pants. You got that?"

His eyes glimmer with something I can't read, at the same time he manages a very sexy, very manly chuckle. The sound is almost sinister and gives me the chills. But the good kind.

I storm away, and as I slam my bedroom door, I hear him full-on laughing.

Fucker.

---

Klaus is going for bonus points. Wherever he's taking me, Dali is allowed to accompany us. She sits in the back of his truck, head out the window, enjoying the heated breeze of summer. *Goofy girl.* Poe, the traitor, was all kinds of nice to Klaus, even sat in his lap. Poe is singular, he likes things his way, and him sitting on Klaus's lap is a true sign of trust from my cat. He isn't one to let just any ol' body pet him, or rub his belly. But he let Nicklaus.

"Where are we going?" I ask. We've been on I-45 for a while now, and we're not headed anywhere towards Dallas, just the opposite. "Um, Klaus…" He doesn't answer. He has his eyes on the road, and he's concentrating. Like really concentrating. His knuckles are fisted around the steering wheel, and his mouth is set in a scowl. "Klaus," I whisper, placing a tentative hand on his thigh. I don't want to startle him, but I have this weird feeling he doesn't like being in a vehicle, that he prefers his bike to an actual car.

His arctic gaze clashes with mine briefly before he turns back to focus on the road.

"Sorry, not a fan of highways."

Aaah, so it was the highway that had him concerned. Not that I blame him; drivers in these parts are insane. To try and take his mind off the road, I talk to him. His answers are clipped, but at least he's talking now.

"Favorite television show?"

"The Walking Dead."

He is so talking my language.

"You?"

"I have a few, but I'll lay them out for you because these are all the types of things that friends should know about one another. Like say, you want to hang out, but you call me on Sunday night, well that right there is a huge no-no. There is *The Walking Dead*, *Game of Thrones*, *The Night Of*. But if you call on Saturday, there's *Outlander* or *Penny Dreadful*. I also like to watch *Ghost Adventures*. But if you call on a Thursday, oh, shit gets real, *The Strain*. And Tuesday is *Agents of Shield*. I usually wait to watch *Vampire Diaries* on Netflix. Just chill at home and well, enjoy my time."

A grin spreads across Klaus's face, and I'm floored.

He has such a beautiful face. It's clear and free of stress right now. Which wasn't the case about five minutes ago.

"So you Netflix and chill?"

"Hells yes, I do," I say out loud and then quickly slap my mouth shut. Fuck. That means something entirely different nowadays. "Wait, that's not what I meant." I backtrack.

"It isn't?" He looks over at me with a raised brow.

"No, I mean, yeah, I watch Netflix, and I do chill, but I don't *Netflix and chill*."

He laughs, and the sound is pleasant and makes my entire body heat with desire. *Bad, Jada. Bad.* I need to not be so *in*to him. Like, at all.

I quickly try and steer the subject to something that won't get me in trouble. Music. I flip on the radio and cringe. Salt N Peppa's, *Let's talk about Sex* is on the radio. Of all the songs that could come on… So I hit the next button, and *Sex on Fire*, by Kings of Leon is just starting up. For the love of cheese and crackers, can I please catch a break?

Klaus finds the entire situation hilarious and doesn't try and hide it.

"I think this is a sign."

I turn and glare at him.

"What? No. That is not a sign."

"Oh, yes, it is, it's saying that we should be friends. Really *good* friends."

I suck my teeth at him before turning my attention to Dali, and I swear, right as I turn my head, she's eyeing both of us. And if dogs can smile, that's what she's doing.

Twenty minutes later, we arrive at our destination. It's a park. Klaus turns off the truck and sits there for a moment before looking over at me. His stare is intense, and his eyes darken. Okay, I'm not going to deny it, we have chemistry, tons, hell, there are enough pheromones floating between us, I'm surprised we haven't reverted to the human version of a mating call. *'Cause right now, I would so answer that call.*

"We're here," he says as if I don't know we've stopped driving.

"I can see that."

He chuckles and places his hand on mine, which is still on his thigh. I had my hand there the entire time.

The *entire* time.

Shit.

I'm so screwed.

Maybe being friends isn't such a good idea. I'm

about to open my mouth and say just that when he leans over and kisses me on the tip of my nose.

"Come on, let's go. I picked out the perfect seats."

Seats?

For what?

I hop out of the cab, and Dali follows, her tail wagging behind her as she keeps pace with Klaus and me. She's on his side, again. My pets are traitors, and although I try and keep distance between Klaus and me, Dali has other ideas. She keeps steering our walk. She's walking in a way where she continuously bumps into Klaus, and in order to avoid being knocked over by my big-ass Lab, he walks closer to me. *Keep it up, Dali girl, and no treats for you.*

I know I don't have pet telepathy, but I like to think my pets and I are synced. I talk to them just as much as they talk to me. We just have a different way of communicating. But Dali is not receiving any of my messages. When I speed up so that Klaus has room, what does he do, why speed up also, of course, and there's Dali, coming up on his left, making sure we stay close together.

"I'm sorry about my dog," I squeak out. *Crap, not the squeaky voice. I do that when I'm over the top nervous or embarrassed.* I try and recover quickly. "She forgot to take her pills this morning."

"She's on medication?" Klaus asks with a serious face.

"Yeah, they're called, 'act right.'"

Again, my sense of humor makes him laugh.

As we near an area with lots of other people, I scan the crowd, and somehow my dick radar is far reaching, because standing not two feet away from us is Jaden. My ex-boyfriend from forever ago, and before I have a chance to do an about face, he spots me.

"Jada, is that you?"

Yeah, douche. As if he doesn't know what I look like. That we're in the same damn area is disappointing. He left Sulphur long before I did. I had no clue he'd be here of all places. It's not Dallas, but it's too close to home for me.

Why can't people just be real, and be like, "Oh, hey, Jada, good to see you again." Only it isn't good to see Jaden again. He's possessive and emotionally abusive. At least he was. Klaus must sense my hesitation because he places an arm over my shoulder and pulls me into his side.

"Jaden," I say in a not-so-friendly way.

Yes, Jada and Jaden, we were like the *it* couple for two years. And people would call us JJ. *Pathetic.* At one time, I thought it was cute. *It's so not cute anymore.*

His face gets that look he used to get so many times before when he was about to cause trouble. But I think he's sizing Klaus up, who happens to be more than a foot taller. *Viking men are awesome.*

"Who's this guy?" Jaden questions. There is definitely anger in his voice, and I can bet you all the money in my wallet right now he is not here alone. Some poor female who probably has no clue the type of man Jaden is, is head-over-heels in love with him. I know she is. I was *that girl* once upon a time.

"I'm Nicklaus. Jada's friend."

"You seem like you're more than friends to me."

"I don't see how that's any of your business, Jaden."

"Anything concerning you is my business. I love you, girl." The word "girl" is said in a high-pitched voice. Almost like it hurts him to say it.

See what I mean?

Crazy train.

Klaus clears his throat and slowly unwraps his arm from my shoulder. His body is tense, and I don't know if he can handle himself, but I suspect he can. He's a Viking, Thor's older half-brother, who is the epitome of all things virile. *Tamp it down, Jada.*

I take a step in front of Klaus, knowing that if the

two of them come to blows, there isn't much I can do, but I try to diffuse the situation anyway.

"Jaden, we are not together, and haven't been for a very long time. Like *years*."

"Yeah, but only because you didn't want to make it work. You shouldn't string men along like that, Jada, it's not right. I did everything I could—"

Cue the girl he actually came with.

"Jada?" the unsuspecting female says.

She's petite, with cute twists in her hair, and has a nose ring. I want to warn her, like really warn her about what she's getting into.

"Liza," Jaden says, red-faced. "This is Jada, and her friend, Klaus."

Liza's eyes go wide, which means she knows who I am.

*Oh, joy.*

There are moments in my life that are just awkward. Like high school awkward, or chick flick awkward. This is one of those moments. I don't know what Jaden has told Liza about me, and I really don't care, but everything happens so fast, I don't even see it coming. Liza starts waving her hands madly in the air, calling me a whore. Dali makes her way in front of me and stands her ground and begins to growl, and

Klaus narrowly misses the punch that Jaden throws his way.

I can't make this shit up.

It really happens.

Liza is all bark and no bite, especially after Dali stands in front of me, but as I move out of the way to get out of punching range of Jaden and Klaus, Dali, my sweet girl, does the unthinkable. She goes in to protect Klaus.

Dogs are smart.

Really smart.

Dali is an agent of Dallas's S.E.E.K. program. It's her job to sniff shit out and go in for the rescue if needed. Unlike other dogs, she knows when she's on or off duty. I try really hard to balance our work/life. So when she goes in to protect Klaus, I'm shocked. Really shocked. Is the universe trying to tell me something? *Amelia, do you really want your husband for me?* And if so, why?

A light breeze whispers across my face at the same moment Klaus grabs Jaden by the collar of his shirt and brings him to his face.

"Your manners are pitiful," he sneers. "To act this way in front of women is wrong." He looks over at Liza, who is in tears. Literally in tears. I look over at her and want to put my bitch face on 'cause I do a good one, but I feel bad for her. I'm outside my element on this, too, as I totally suck when it comes to awkward confrontations. I'm the one who thinks of something witty to say two hours after the incident is over.

"Liza, I don't know what Jaden told you, but we haven't been together for more than six years, and the reason for that is because he's a liar and an abuser. You really need to find someone else, he's no good."

"You don't know what you're talking about." Typical. Can't tell people anything.

"Yeah, I kind of do. I'm an expert when it comes to assholes." I shrug and bend low to get Dali's attention. Liza will have to learn on her own.

"Good job, girl," I say to Dali.

Someone must have called the police because there's an officer walking towards us and he doesn't look happy.

"What seems to be the problem here?"

Klaus still has Jaden by the collar but turns in the direction of the officer.

"This man tried to assault me and my friend."

The officer looks over at me, and I know him. It's Officer Bledsoe.

"Jada, why am I not surprised?"

"What?" I shrug. "You act like I'm a magnet for trouble."

"Woman, you so are. What about six months ago, at the Golden Corral?"

Okay, there was an incident at the Golden Corral, but it wasn't my fault. The guy wouldn't stop talking and kept trying to sit at my table. All I did was toss my drink on him. It was mostly by accident. I got flustered, and my nerves were shot to shit that day.

"That wasn't my fault."

"Right, you couldn't just say 'go away?'" Officer Bledsoe asks.

"I did. Like a million times." Then my drink had wings and flew and landed on the guy who kept trying to talk to me.

Bledsoe looks at Jaden, who's now been released by my Viking savior.

"Are you going to be a problem?"

"No," Jaden hisses.

"Good. Now, you go this way, and, Jada, you and your friend go that way."

"That's all we were trying to do."

Klaus takes my hand, and I let him. When we reach an area with lawn chairs, he has a smile on his face and starts waving at someone in the crowd. It's

Tammy and a couple of other people I've not met before. I pull on Klaus's hand to get his attention.

"Your friends don't think we're dating, do they?"

His smile widens.

"Do you want them to think we're dating?"

"No," I gasp. "We're friends, just friends."

"Who are you trying to convince, Jada? You, or me?"

Now wasn't that the real question of the day.

5

---

Tammy is the first one to greet me.

"Girl, don't you look spiffy."

I'm not dressed to the nines or anything. I'm in jean shorts and a racerback tank. It's hotter than Hades, and I wasn't sure what we were doing. When I came from changing, Klaus hadn't said I needed to rethink my outfit so I assumed it was okay. Tammy is dressed similarly; she's wearing jean shorts, a halter top with rhinestones, and her cowboy boots. Everyone in the group is hugged up with someone, and I turn to look up at Klaus as I scowl.

"They *do* think we're a couple," I hiss.

He steps closer to me, and again, there is laughter in his eyes, but he doesn't say anything. He tags me around the waist, pulling me in front of him, and with a loud voice, filled with laughter, he yells to the crowd.

"Everyone, this is Jada, and she wants you all to know that we're not dating, that we're only friends."

"With benefits, I hope," someone shouts.

This can't be happening, but I can't stop the smile that spreads across my face.

His head is resting on my shoulder now, and in my ear, he whispers in that deep accented voice, "You happy now, sunshine?"

"Supremely," I say smugly.

"Good." He kisses my cheek lightly and releases me. Not even a full second later, I wish he hadn't.

We're at a barbeque slash park concert. There is a local band playing that I've not heard of before, and some guy everyone calls Chops is grilling steaks and corn on a massive grill. He's got a full beard and wears a thick bandana across his forehead. His sunglasses make him look cool, like way too cool. It's obvious Klaus's friends are bikers; and as much as I'd like to say I feel out of place, I don't. Neither does Dali. She sticks to either my or Klaus's side. She's playful and in good spirits. Not unusual for my Dali girl, but it makes me smile to see her so carefree.

"So, girl, what are your intentions with Nicklaus over there." Chops gestures over to where Klaus is standing with a red solo cup in his hand, talking to some other guys.

"My intentions?"

"Yeah, girl. Intentions."

"Well, I guess to be a good friend."

Chops tilts his head down at me, and I'm reminded that most of the men here are mountainous. Like ginormous, and they could all be superheroes.

"So, a good friend. Never seen one of them before dressed like you, looking like you do. Your eyes give you away, girl."

"Excuse me?"

"Your eyes, girl. They don't lie. You want him, and you want him bad. I'm just trying to figure out what your play is."

*My play?*

"I don't have a play," I tell Chops.

At that, he grunts.

"All women have some sort of play. It's in your handbook that's handed down from mother to daughter via the womb."

I place my hands on my hips and am about to tell Chops about himself when he barks out a surprised laugh.

"Oh, and you got some fire in you. *Muy caliente.*"

*Muy caliente?*

I can't help it. I burst out laughing, because badass biker dude just said *muy caliente*.

"You have a pass for now, girl, but just so you know, I'm not judging, only making an observation. This is the first time Klaus has brought anyone here with him. Last time he came with a woman, it was his Amelia and their son. So you tread carefully, because although you can't tell, I'm the bad guy out of the group, and I have no problem laying into you if you hurt my brother."

I don't know if Chops is trying to scare me, but it isn't working. And I let him know.

"Well, Chops, I'd just like you to know that if you ever do decide to lay into me, I'm a uniformed officer of the law, which means not only will I exercise my right as said officer, I have no problem taking your ass out."

Then, I turn and show him my service pistol.

His eyes go wide for a moment. The surly bastard bursts into more laughter. This time, loud and booming, making everyone within hearing range turn in our direction.

"Yeah, girl. You'll fit in here quite well. Now, fix your man a plate, he's hungry."

When did Klaus become "my man?"

I do fix Klaus a plate, but that does not mean he's mine. I sit in between his legs as we eat off the same plate and give our bones to Dali, but it doesn't mean we're a couple. We're just two people hanging out as friends. *Keep telling yourself that.* It's true. Tammy and her guy Hector come over, and the four of us decide it would be a good idea to go to the river the following weekend.

"What about the farm?" Klaus asks.

"Thomas takes care of the farm. I have no clue what I'm doing."

"You have a farm?" Tammy asks.

"Yeah, eventually going to fill it with animals and things."

"Well, hell, girl, why don't we all come to your place next weekend and have a steak and potato grill night."

Normally, it would rankle my nerves that someone would just invite themselves over. But sitting here and feeling comfortable like I do, I actually don't have a problem with it, so I agree.

"Sure, I have to work a double shift Friday, but if you don't mind grilling later in the evening, it's doable."

"Perfect."

Tammy stands, dusting her shorts off, and hollers to the crowd.

"Guys, steak and potato grill at Jada's farm next weekend."

Everyone yells their acceptance.

Shit.

I thought it was just going to be the four of us.

"Hey," Klaus's voice rumbles in my ear, his breath warm against my cheek. "You don't want to do this, just say so, and I'll tell everyone to back off."

Well, it was too late for that. Plus, I don't want his friends to think I'm flighty. Or not sociable.

"No, it's fine. This is what friends do, right? Hang out."

"Yeah. I'm pulling a seventy-two-hour shift at the station. Be done Wednesday. You mind if I come over Thursday, we can shop for the steaks and potatoes."

We were shopping together now?

How the hell had that happened?

"Um, sure."

"Good."

The stubble on his chin scratches my shoulder, and I feel like he's doing it on purpose, but I don't call him out on it.

The ride home takes forever. I've been reflective, a little moody, and basically just confused. Klaus is my dead best friend's widowed husband, and it's bothering me to the point that I'm not very good company.

"You were much more talkative at the park and on the way there than you are now."

It's because my mind is a mess.

"Why would Amelia tell you I was good for you?" I blurt.

"Because that's just the way she was. Trust me, I had no intention of ever seeking you out. I was just in Sulphur to see her parents. Didn't plan on you happening. But you did."

"Don't you see how messed up it would be if we did get together?"

He turns to look at me as he pulls the car into my drive and shuts off the engine.

"I think it's only messed up if we let it be messed up. I'm not declaring my undying love for you and vice versa. But if we happen to spend time together, at least we both know she'd have been okay with it."

Gah, this is so screwed up.

I try unbuckling my seatbelt and find that I'm

stuck. I can't get free. Klaus leans over at the same time I do, and we bump heads. Jerking back, I place my hand on my forehead because, damn, the brother has a serious noggin.

His hands are warm against the side of my hip as he messes with the belt buckle, and my chest constricts. I was okay at the park. Totally fine. But now inside the cab of his truck, I'm about to have a serious panic attack. I haven't had a panic attack in years. Dali senses my frustration and starts to whine.

"It's okay, girl. Just gotta get your momma unstuck. She's managed to get a piece of her shirt caught in with the belt buckle."

Of course, I have.

I'm Jada Alexander, and apparently, I'm accident-prone. *Only around him.*

Klaus pulls a knife from the cup holder in the dash.

"Sorry, but the shirt must die," he informs me.

"Fine."

He looks up at me with those amazing eyes of his, and I can't help it. I melt. He doesn't say anything further as he cuts my shirt away, setting me free of the belt buckle. Of course, once he does that, the buckle pops loose, and viola, torn shirt equals rescued Jada.

"Don't move," he says, and my breath halts. He's

so close, *too* close, but still, the right amount of close where I get a whiff of him. It's all downhill for my libido from there. I'm moving closer, and he's moving closer. This is all too much for me to handle. There are a million things running through my mind at this moment, and surprisingly, they aren't comic book or movie related. Right when I think he's about to kiss me, he sits back and opens his car door. "I'll walk you to your door."

*You'll walk me to my door?*

Walk me.

To my door.

For fuck's sake. I was so sure we were about to be fogging up the damn car. *No, you're not getting involved with him.* My mind screams at me, but my body, well, the lust-crazed lunatic that she is, is telling me to get down on it. Yeah, I'm singing Kool in the Gang. Okay, my subconscious is. My mind is telling me no, but my body's telling me yes. *I don't see nothing wrong...* Stop! Stop! Stop! And that, that was R. Kelly. I'm a wreck.

Like an idiot, I wait for him to open the car door. As he does, he stands in front of me, blocking any chance I have of getting out of the vehicle.

"Can't get down unless you move out of the way."

"I said I'd help you." His hands go to my waist,

and he lifts me out of the truck. If it wasn't confirmed then, it's official now, Nicklaus is a Viking. A strong, strapping Viking of a man, and I want to swoon all over his hot body like melted butter.

"You can put me down now," I say as he grips my waist.

"I could, but I'm not going to."

"Why?" I croak. I sound like one of those needy girls. This is what one would call tension. Hot, sexy tension. We're practically pressed against each other like peanut butter and jam. His hard body molded to my soft curves.

"I think," he says softly, "that we are fooling ourselves if we really think that being friends is the right thing to do."

"You do?" I ask, and yeah, it's the voice, the one where you know the guy's right, but you play dumb anyway.

"Yeah, I do. And I think you know that, too."

"I do?"

His face is getting closer to mine; any closer and there will be lip service. Serious lip service.

"You want to know what else I think," he rumbles.

"Uh hunn." Lost, desperate, hot voice of need. That's what that sound is.

"I think that if I were to kiss you right now, you'd let me."

My brain short circuits at this point because he basically *is* kissing me. That last word "me" was said against my lips. I can't help it, I want to taste his words, so I push forward against his lips, and say," I think you might be right."

That's all it takes.

Nothing else is said because there isn't anything else left to say. Before I can even drop the 't' in "right," his tongue is in my mouth. No excuses, no permission, it's all invasion. His tongue goes in for the kill, and his mouth devours mine. Conquers me like the Viking he is. Hot, soft, wet, warm, those words don't do this man's mouth any damn justice at all. And the kiss? Well, it's explosive. I'm trapped in between the car and this mountain of a man, and he has the good sense to keep his hand pressed against my back so that the car doesn't become a part of my skin. I give just as good as he gives, if not better.

We're talking intergalactic planetary, planetary, intergalactic. *And you just quoted a song to compare a kiss, Jada,* I hiss inside my head as I try and fail to get a grip on the situation. Klaus kisses like I'm the only thing in his world, that if they were to drop nukes right now, he wouldn't stop, because this is where he'd want to be when he died. With me. Holding me, kissing me, consuming me like he has every right, because he owns me.

*Oh, I so want to be owned.*

I'd gladly turn in my single rewards loyalty card for a Nicklaus loyalty card. His swagger tank's on full, and let's face it, any man that can work you up so high and bring you crashing down in a puddle of lust deserves your loyalty. Don't get it twisted, some men can fake a good kiss, but we know. We know if it's the real deal because we can feel it in our bones. Down to the pit of our souls, there is this switch that gets hit when the guy—*the* guy—gets it right. You don't get many chances to find someone you can vibe with on this level. It's rare.

You get maybe, one, two shots tops at it. I've never had a shot like this before, so I don't know what else to do but see it for what it really is. Right?

Right.

I'm thinking all this, and mind you, we haven't even come up for air. Not yet. And I don't care if my lungs start to burn, I don't want to breathe again. Not ever. But Klaus pulls away and he's tugging me toward the house, where Dali waits patiently by the door. *When had she gotten out of the car?*

"Keys, Jada."

Oh, right. We need to get inside.

I fumble with my bag, and Klaus's hand wraps gently around mine as I grab hold of the keys that somehow get lost in my itty-bitty purse. His hand goes to my stomach, and he gently pushes me back as he opens my door. This doesn't happen, like ever. Poe is in the middle of the hall, his green eyes are glowing, and instead of hissing at the male guest, he stands, stretches and walks towards my room, as if he's actually leading the procession.

My animals have lost their damn minds.

*So have I.*

Because we're headed straight for my room. A place he hasn't seen yet, and I'm a bit scared, 'cause Thor and his band of men have leading roles in my bedroom décor. Strong hands tug at my hips and pull me against his hard body, and I'm lost in the kiss again. This time, the kiss goes on and on. We're speaking an entirely new language and it's all hands, mouths, teeth and tongue. Even our sounds have their own meanings, and we moan each one in harmony. Mine is more of a contralto, where as his are deeper, throatier than mine. My legs hit the back of the bed, and I instantly grab hold of Klaus's waist so I don't fall.

"I got you," Klaus rumbles against my lips, and

he's right. He does have me. Right where he wants me. My hands slide up his sides, and his shirt rises, giving me a glimpse of a very bold, very sexy tattoo that starts below the waistband of his pants and travels up beneath his right armpit. I can't really see what it is, but I can tell its badass. "We have to slow down," he warns.

Slow down?

What? Why?

"I don't know if you've noticed, Klaus, but I'm way past the point of slow."

His throaty chuckle causes my stomach to flutter.

"We just got back in touch, I don't want to ruin this. We owe it to ourselves to see if there's really something between us."

Uh. Duh.

Of course, there's something between us. He has a large, hard cock between my legs, and I'm hot, wet, and for the love of all that is holy, ready.

"I don't want anything between us. Just skin on skin," I tease.

This causes Klaus to untangle himself from me and step back. He's eyeing me with a funny look on his face.

My lips are swollen from his kisses, and I know

my hair is a hot ass mess. What more can a guy ask for?

"Jada. Gorgeous. I'm more than willing to take us all the way there, but you're not ready."

"Not ready?"

I'm about to show him my underwear to prove he's wrong when it hits me.

Mother. Fuck.

I'm wearing granny panties, with a capital G!

How in the hell did I forget I was wearing the big-girl drawers?

How!

"Not yet."

My shoulders deflate. Not because of his words, even though, in a way, he's right. Yesterday, I was all about keeping us friendly, but now, I'm mortified. What if he'd tried to go down on me while I was wearing my bloomers? I'm not going to think about that. I can't. It's too embarrassing. And where the hell is Dali? Why isn't she interrupting our tryst?

"You're right."

He looks surprised.

"I am."

"Of course, you're right. We need to get to know each other. Find out what makes the other tick. See if we're good at even being friends before we can be lovers. I'm down with that plan."

He doesn't say anything for a long time.

"I don't want to be your friend, Jada," he grumps.

"What do you want to be, Klaus?"

He rakes his hands through his beautiful hair. Did I mention his hair is overly long? Long enough for a decent man-bun. All that beautiful hair, I can't wait to get my fingers in it. And his facial scruff. Lordy, lordy ,lordy. I don't think anyone should be denied the pleasure of a good roughing up with facial hair like that.

"To be honest, I don't really know. I like you, and yes, I'd love nothing more than to strip you out of your outfit, feast on your body, and have you screaming my name until your throat gets raw, but I don't want to ruin this either."

"So let's not ruin it. Let's take it slow."

He steps forward and takes my hands in his.

"Slow is good."

"Slow is good," I repeat.

"I'll call you when I get home."

"Okay," I huff.

Klaus grins. He knows I'm not happy with the decision we both sort of made, and he's trying to make light of it. I'm about to tell him about himself when he pulls me back in for another belly clincher of a kiss.

"I'll call you tonight, gorgeous."

"Tonight," I whisper, placing my fingers over my lips, which are still tingling.

6

Klaus calls exactly forty-five minutes later. Yes, I timed it. I answer on the first ring. I'm not one to play the 'let it ring some more' game. It's not who I am. Okay, maybe I *was* that person a long time ago, but not anymore.

"Hey," I say into the phone.

"Hey." His voice caresses my ear, and I feel it between my thighs. "You getting ready for bed?" he asks me.

"No."

"Why not?"

"I have some things I need to finish up at the house. I didn't realize we were going to be gone all day."

"Sorry I kept you from your other things."

He had nothing to be sorry for.

"Oh, no, it's not like that, Klaus. Honest."

"I like your phone voice," he says, changing the subject.

"Oh, really?" I say playfully.

"Yes. Really. It's smooth, throaty. I can feel it. It's almost as if you're touching me." His voice drops to a harsh whisper. "Everywhere."

Oh, boy. So can I.

"Feeling's mutual."

"Glad to hear it. What do you need to finish up?"

"Well, I need to give Poe his vitamins. Dali gets a bath on Sundays, and then I need to finish my report."

I was going to get in a lot of trouble if I didn't have my report in regarding what I found at the fire. Dali hadn't found anything truly worth reporting, but I still needed to be detailed.

"From the fire a couple of days ago?"

"Yeah."

"Well, you're smart, you'll get it sorted."

"Thanks," I say, and I mean it. The last guy I attempted to have any sort of relationship with thought me working for the ATF was a joke. He didn't outright say it, but he'd insinuated it plenty of times. I dropped his ass like a bad habit on Sunday.

Dali places her head in my lap, and that's my signal. It's bath time.

"Klaus, I gotta go. Dali's ready for her bath."

"Okay, I'll see you Thursday."

"Wait, you're gonna call, right?"

He chuckles over the phone.

"Yeah, gorgeous, I'm calling you. It may be at odd times, though. But what time do you usually get home from work?"

"It really just depends on what cases are on my desk, or if any new ones come across. On a good day, I'm normally home by six."

"All right, I'll see what I can do."

"'Night, Klaus."

"'Night, Jada."

7

It's Tuesday. Freaking Tuesday. I haven't heard one word from Klaus. I've been staring at my phone for what seems likes hours, and I refuse to be the stalker. *Do not text him. Do not text him.* That's the mantra playing over and over inside my head. Why hasn't he called? I know he's working a triple, but a simple text is not hard. Your fingers just fly over the screen, and you press Send. That's it, it's not rocket science.

It's hot out today. It's the kind of hot mixed with humidity that makes you feel like you're in a perpetual sauna. But because I don't want to keep the fur babies inside all day, I decide to make a light salad with some chicken tossed in and eat on the back deck. I also brew up the best batch of sweet tea this side of the Mississippi. I take in my yard and my Dali girl as she lounges on the bottom step of the patio. Poe lounges in the shade, staring longingly at the window, wanting to go inside. Poe is a bit of a snob. But that's why I adore him so much. He makes sure his thoughts don't go unanswered.

Thomas mended the fence on the south end of the property, and I can see him coming in for the evening.

"Hey, Thomas," I call out.

"Hey, Jada."

He gets closer, and as he moves up the steps, I offer him a seat. Thomas is taller than me, maybe almost six feet, but not quite. He has kind eyes and is easy to talk to. Since he moved to the ranch, I've not seen him bring anyone home, and I don't think he's seeing anyone. Men usually have a certain aura about them when they're in a serious relationship. He doesn't have that at all.

"You want me to fix you a plate?"

"Nah, I'm gonna go have dinner with my cousin."

My head turns in his direction.

"I didn't know you had family out this way?"

Come to think of it, there isn't much I *do* know about him, except that he came highly recommended by the realtor when I bought the place.

"He's visiting for a while. Came to scope out the scene, see if it's somewhere he wants to move to."

"Well, that's great. You should invite him over to your place."

"Yeah, maybe. He's not much for ranch life, though."

I laugh.

"Neither am I, but look at me now." I gesture out at all the land in front of us. I don't have any animals on the farm yet, but I plan to. Really soon. I just have to get things situated the way I want, and then I plan to open this place up and give ranching a go.

Thomas laughs.

"Yeah, look at you now."

He stands, tells me goodnight, and then he's gone. Dali is running around in the yard, and Poe is perched on the rail. He has a serious look in his green eyes, and he's staring straight at me.

"What now?" I ask my cat.

Poe dips his head and turns in Dali's direction.

"No one said you had to stay on the porch."

I swear my cat looks at me as if to say he's too good to frolic and thinks Dali is wasting her time running around like a crazy person.

"Whatevs, Poe. You sit there. I'm gonna go play

catch with Dali. You better hope a hawk doesn't spot you. I hear cats are on the menu in these parts."

Poe hisses at me.

See, my animals totally understand what I'm saying.

Before I can even get the ball out from the trunk of toys I have stashed on the deck, my phone rings. I don't look to see who it is, just answer.

"Hello."

"Dude!"

It's Caroline, and she's screaming in my ear.

"What?" I say back.

"I'm like, not even five minutes from your pad. It's Wednesday night, I say we get our asses out and do some dancing."

I groan into the phone. This is my best friend, and I love her, but she seriously needs to take her life down a notch.

"I have work tomorrow."

"So?"

Typical Caroline.

"So…I have to get up in the morning. Some of us have regular jobs."

Caroline is smart. She's a ball buster, and up until last year, she was going to school to get her degree in criminal law. But she dropped out all of sudden. No word, nothing. She won't even talk about what happened to her while she was away at college. She gets moody, and instead of making her talk about it, I let her get away with bloody murder, which is why I'm going to my room to find something to wear. I'd rather just chill at my house, but she won't go for it.

"Come on, Jada, be my wingman."

"Really? You hurting that bad?"

"Nah, not really, just want some guy to feel me up so I can feel good about myself," she half-jokes. That's how I know something really bad happened to her while she was away at school.

"You do know if you talk about it, it will get easier."

"Yeah, well, it will never get easier, and the only way I can cope is on the dance floor, or with a bottle of Crown. Wouldn't you rather I just dance it off?"

"Yeah, babe, I would."

She screams into my ear before hanging up.

Not even ten minutes later, she's walking through my door all done up and ready to catch some bees with her honey. I haven't mentioned Klaus to her. There just hasn't been enough time, and that's when I decide that maybe going out isn't such a bad idea. *It will get your mind off Klaus.*

Because he definitely isn't calling.

Caroline chooses a club I know well. It's loud, and I can already smell the sweat and alcohol in the air. The DJ is playing Black Eyed Peas, and my friend wastes no time announcing that this is her jam. I take hold of her hand so we don't get separated. It's too crowded, and all I can think is that the building is so not up to code. There is only one exit, and there should be at least two additional ways out, and the ventilation inside is horrible. The air is thick, and I swear at any minute, people will start dropping like flies from heat exhaustion.

We start dancing. Caroline throws her entire body into her moves and makes it look like she's more than available to the men watching. I try and keep to myself. I'm not really feeling tonight. I can't help but wonder why Klaus hasn't called. I didn't do anything wrong. I sure as hell didn't send out the wrong signal. At least, I don't think I did. The song switches to Drake's *Hotline Bling,* and that's when I turn around to leave the floor and run right into my ex. *Can someone up there please give me a break?* It's like there is a drama cloud overhead, following me around in an eternal episode of Jerry Springer's worst possible scenario moments.

"I thought that was you."

Ugh.

Can I just say that the expression, "I threw up a little in my mouth" is a real thing, it's not just an expression. That shit really happens.

"Jaden."

"What are you doing here by yourself?" Jaden asks as if he's truly concerned.

"I'm not alone, and it's none of your business."

'Everything you do is my business, Jada. When are you going to realize that?"

"Can we just not do this? I'm exhausted. I don't want to deal with you right now."

"Deal with me?" The music is loud, but I can tell he's getting angry. The vein on his forehead is starting to bulge.

Shit.

I don't have time for a scene.

"Jaden, you need to turn around and walk the other way."

He grins at me, and it's not a nice grin either. I don't know how long we stand there, but the lights get dimmer as Drake's song ends, and The Weeknd's *Can't Feel My Face* starts going. Caroline takes that moment to realize the situation I'm in when she stops next to me.

"Jaden, what are you doing here?"

"Caroline, I didn't know they let your type in."

"Fuck you, Jaden."

"You've already done that, Caroline." He smirks.

I can't hear the music anymore. Maybe because I'm in shock.

This is news to me.

I look at Caroline. Her eyes are big, and her bottom lip is quivering. I know Caroline like the back of my hand. I know all her tells.

"Seriously, Caroline?"

"Jada, let me explain."

I shake my head. I'm too angry, but not because I have residual feelings for Jaden. I have nothing but love for Caroline, and for her to have slept with my ex, well…that is just wrong on all kinds of levels. She might as well have just shoved a big *Fuck You* sign in my face.

I turn to leave when she grabs my wrist.

"You don't want to do that, Caroline. Not right now," I yell over the music.

"You don't understand, Jada. I was drunk."

"Right, and let me guess, you didn't know what you were doing? Am I right?"

"Oh, she knew what she was doing," Jaden adds.

"Shut up! Shut up!" Caroline yells over the music.

"I'm out of here."

I push past gyrating bodies, and my face is hot from embarrassment and…wet.

Am I crying?

Shit.

I am.

*Stop it, Jada. This isn't going to be the last time someone hurts you.*

This is all too much for me. It sounds lame, right? Well, for me, it isn't. I can't help but feel the way I feel. I trusted her. Confided in her all my aches and pains when it came to Jaden. If anyone knows what type of monster he is, it's her. She witnessed some of his greatest fuck-ups firsthand.

Caroline is supposed to be my go-to gal. My best friend. Why would she hang out with Jaden anyway? I don't get it. Why keep it from me. She should have come clean. *She knew you'd be mad.* Well, duh. Of course, I'm mad. I don't do the 'you sleep with my boyfriend, and I'll sleep with yours after you're done' game. That's not cool on so many levels.

When I finally make it outside, I take a deep breath and get myself back together. But the gods of fate and fuck-ups are not done with me. I laugh almost hysterically as I realize I came with Caroline, in her car. I'm not going back in there. No way. I pull my cell from my purse and call for an Uber. I walk off to the side of the building and wait for my ride when I notice a motorcycle. Not just any bike, but a Dyna. It looks just like Klaus's. Exactly like his, actually. It's parked at the coffee shop next to the bar, and I can see the occupants inside clearly. Klaus is inside, sitting down at a table and there is a woman sitting across from him.

They are in a serious conversation, and their hands are clasped. Have I mentioned I'm not one for drama? I don't do drama. I've lived it, breathed it, and had Jerry Springer on speed-dial. Plus, I'm the girl that clams up when it comes to personal confrontation. I get all tongue-tied. Sometimes I'm able to get my words out, but when it comes to total devastation—like now—I'm struck dumb. I'm about to turn away, but before I can, I'm blinded by the lights from a large Ford F-350. It gets the attention of the occupants inside the diner because when my vision finally clears, Klaus is staring straight at me.

I'm frozen to the spot.

All I can do is stare back.

It's obvious he didn't call me because he was spending his time with the woman across from him. Why does this always happen to me? Like, how is it that I manage to get it wrong, every single time? *We're not in a relationship*, I remind myself. All we did is kiss. He's not married, and maybe he's done with the whole monogamous thing. So the girl in the shop must be his other side piece. No, that's not right. *I'm the side piece. Bingo.*

I don't cause a scene, and maybe that's what Klaus expects. Instead, I give him a chin lift, and just like in the movies, before he can even acknowledge me, a car pulls up, and it's the Uber I called. *Perfect timing.* I get inside and keep my conversation to a minimum. I just want to get home, take a long bath, and read the new M.L. Olson book.

---

The moment I get home, I toss my bag on the floor by the door, step out of my shoes, walk to my bathroom, and start my bath. I'm on autopilot. I don't even remember how I made it out of my clothes and into the tub. The heat from the water calms my nerves, but only for a handful of moments. I start to take big gulps of air into my lungs. *I'm not going to freak out.* I'm not. I have no ties to any of them. Not a one. Jaden and Caroline can fuck like rabbits until the sun comes up for all I care, and well, Klaus and I aren't exclusive, we aren't even a couple, he made it clear he wanted to take things slow. Maybe his idea of slow is a steady girlfriend while he strings me along on the side.

My phone is ringing, but I let it go to voicemail. It's by the front door anyway. It's probably Caroline. It isn't Klaus, that's for sure. He has to know he can't call me, not now, not after three days of complete silence. My phone rings again and again. It's not the work phone, so I'm in the clear. When I finally pull myself out of the tub, I grab my Kindle and make my way over to my reading nook.

I barely swipe the screen on my tablet when there is a loud knock at my door. Dali's ears perk up, and she's up, following me as I make my way to the front door.

"Jada, can you open the door please."

Klaus.

"Why are you here?" I say through the wood.

"You didn't answer your phone. I got worried."

I almost laugh.

"Well, I'm fine. You can go now."

"Jada, open up. I know you saw me."

"Yeah, I know, you know I saw you." *Wow, people actually say that?* I would laugh if this situation were funny.

"So, open up so I can explain."

Explain? What was there to explain?

"There's nothing to explain, Klaus. I have no ties to you."

"Open the door, Jada." His voice is stern. He even sounds exasperated, like he's tired of having to explain his actions.

"If I open up and let you explain, will you go away?"

"No."

"No? Why the hell not?"

"'Cause that's not what either of us wants."

"Speak for yourself."

I hear a *thud* sound. Like he's face-planted into my door. I know if I open the door, things are not going to get any better; hell, they may even get worse. Do I really want worse right now?

I fling open the door, and the first thing I notice is Klaus's sharp intake of breath, the second is that his eyes are blazing blue fire.

I look down and realize I've done it again. I'm practically naked. What is it with me and answering the door for him with barely any clothes on?

"I'll be right back."

I run to my room and throw on a pair of sweats. When I come back out, he's in the kitchen, making a pot of tea.

"What do you think you're doing?"

"Making us some tea."

"Why?"

"Because you look like you could use some."

"I don't recall asking for any."

"Didn't say you asked. Now, sit so I can explain."

I reluctantly slide into the stool at the bar in my kitchen.

Neither of us says anything for a long period of time.

"That wasn't what it looked like."

"Says every man who's been caught red-handed."

"Jada, you didn't catch me at anything. You just happened to witness something that looked one way, but was actually another."

"How do you figure that?"

Klaus pulls down two cups from my cupboard and rubs Dali on the back of the head. She lets him, too. She's all about kissing Klaus's ass. *Traitor dog.*

"Well, the woman in the diner is a friend."

"I gathered as much." I try to put on my game face, but remember, personal confrontation and I go hand in hand about as well as lemon juice and cuts.

"She's Chops' old lady."

Chops' old lady.

"Okay."

"She and Chops are thinking of having a baby, and she knows about my situation. So does Chops. They're just scared. She wanted to know if I thought having a kid was a bad idea."

"What did you tell her?"

"I told her if she didn't have a kid, then that in itself would be a bad idea because she and Chops will make terrific parents."

Now, what do I say?

I sigh loudly. How can I be mad about that? Then I remember, I haven't heard from him in three days, and I want to be angry all over again. *He works at the station.* Yeah, he does. But he's the mechanic.

"Are you going to say anything?" He asks while handing me a steaming cup of tea. He's chosen my Blueberry Merlot, which happens to be one of my favorites. I take a sip, and my shoulders slouch a bit. I hunch over my cup and take a deep breath before looking up at Klaus.

"What do you want me to say?" I ask, instead of saying what's really on my mind.

"You can say whatever you want, Jada. Just don't shut me out."

"Why? You act like we're in some kind of relationship, and we're not. You and I both decided that it would be ideal to take things slow."

He stands taller and rounds the counter to come to stand in front of me. His eyes are searching mine. The dark orbs of his eyes are intense. He goes from my eyes to my mouth before cursing under his breath. Next thing I feel are his lips coming down on mine and my mind immediately shuts down as my body takes over. It's like zero to one-hundred in a handful of seconds. I had no clue my body could get that hot, that fast. *It's because I'm sex deprived,* I try and rationalize as his tongue sweeps into my mouth and proceeds to own me. My hands go to his waist, and my fingers hook into the loops of his jeans. I tug him between my legs. It's exactly where he belongs. There is a slight grunt from Klaus, then he's right back to owning my mouth.

Ladies, have you ever been so possessed by a kiss, that you forget your own name? I can't form a single coherent thought. My mind is completely wiped clean of all the reasons I want to be mad at him. All my original complaints seem so trivial. His kiss is better than the one delivered by Ryan Gosling to Rachel McAdams in *The Notebook*. Let's face it, we all want a man to deliver *that* kind of kiss and more. Klaus knocks it out of the fucking ballpark and into the next stratosphere. His jeans sit low on his hips, and I can feel the heated skin just above his waistline.

My hands suddenly have a mind of their own. Somehow, I end up standing. Really, it's truly a miracle how I even managed to not fall down because my hands go up his sides, taking his shirt with me, and we separate for a second. Long enough for me to remove the offending material. I freeze.

Yes.

Freeze.

His body is, well, it is… A fucking work of art. There are scars, there is ink, and there is muscle stacked on muscle. Deep shadows contour the features of his overly defined abs. I have to admit, I'm no shrinking violet. I'm in good fucking shape. But he puts my body to shame. I inwardly groan because I started this. Wait, no, he did. I just took it a step further. But before I can attempt to blame my actions on my out of practice libido, Klaus has my back to his front and is pinning me to the counter in front of us. His arm bands diagonally around my stomach and chest as his other hand wraps around my throat.

*Kinky.*

His lips kiss my shoulder, neck, and the underside of my jaw, as the hand around my throat positions my head the way he wants. His hands are multi-talented; one controls the movement of my head, giving him better access to my neck. The other hand has a firm hold on my waist and guides my ass into his erection. The entire time this is happening, I feel as if I'm going to die because there's not enough air circulating in my lungs. I can't seem to catch my breath fast enough. Let's put this encounter on pause for a second and let me explain a few things. First off, I've not properly gotten off with a man in a very long time. Second, and let's be honest here, taking matters into your own hands only goes so far, which leads me to my third point. I've only read about shit like this in books. You know, where the female can orgasm just from a man's touch alone. Up until this very moment in time, I didn't realize it was a possible reality and not just fantasy. Because holy shit, Batman, I just went off like a rocket. Yes, I was coaxed into the most intense orgasm of my entire life. Klaus is a god among men, and I haven't dated very many men to even make that kind of call, but who gives a fuck.

"Oh, God!" I cry out.

"Klaus," he grunts.

My mind is too clouded to understand what the hell he's talking about. My body shudders uncontrollably, and whatever strength I had in my legs is gone. Completely gone. I try to compose myself as my body goes limp. The arm across my body gets tighter, and I hear his voice in my ear.

"Next time you come, you scream my name, gorgeous."

There's going to be a next time?

*Oh goody.*

There is no appropriate etiquette for how to properly behave when a man, or should I say god, kisses you so thoroughly and touches you so completely that your body ceases to function properly. I know I keep referring to him as Thor's older half-brother, but I don't know how else to give a proper comparison. Klaus is dark and unforgiving in his touches. I feel things because of him; things I don't normally feel, and I don't know how to hide it. I can't keep my composure around him, and when he turns me to face him, I know he can see the naked truth written all over my face.

I am in the sweetest hell because there is a one hundred percent probability that I'm falling for my dead best friend's widower.

*Amelia, how could you leave this beautiful man?*

This gorgeous man is broken. Scarred. There is no wrong or right answer in this kind of scenario.

As I look up at him, I can see it in his eyes. He's hesitant with me, which leads me to believe that what I've just experienced with him isn't even the icing on the cake. *I'm in so much trouble.*

His fingers go to my chin, and he lifts my face up to receive his kiss. I still have to stand on my toes to even reach his mouth properly. I want to say Klaus is selfish for not meeting me halfway, but something tells me he's not selfish at all. Something tells me this is a test. A test brought to you by the emergency broadcast system of Nicklaus. Maybe he wants to see if I'm willing to take this to the next level.

Am I even ready for some next-level shit?

My body screams. *Yes, yes you are!*

He's not wearing a shirt.

I'm still fully clothed.

The erection in his pants is digging into my stomach now. This kiss is sweeter. Slower. His lips move over mine gently, feather-soft. The stroke of his tongue is lazy and warm. The flavor of his kiss is bold and is the perfect combination of sweet and spicy. My entire body starts to hum. He's building me up again, ready to set me on fire. When the kiss finally ends, every single cell in my body is alive and firing on all cylinders. *Jada's log, sexdate 1591.1 My position, orbiting somewhere between dazed and confused.*

Shit. I'm getting nervous. I'm quoting *Star Trek*.

Our eyes lock in an intense stare. My breathing kicks up a notch, and I'm kind of worried that he's remained too calm through this entire ordeal.

"Klaus?" I whisper. "Say something."

He doesn't.

He just stares at me. His eyes roam over my face. His fingers remain at my chin, then lower, and finally, he takes a step back.

"Fuck," he whispers harshly. "I'm ruining this."

What? No!

"How?"

"I said I wanted to take this slow."

He turns, picks his shirt up off the counter, and quickly tosses it back on. To say I'm speechless is an understatement.

I'm way beyond pissed. Or so stimulated rather, I'm about two seconds from throwing a fit.

"Are you serious right now?"

He has to be because no guy in the history of guydom would ever turn down free ass. Like *ever*. My heart is now beating erratically for an entirely different reason.

"Jada, I'm sorry. I got carried away."

"Carried away?"

I walk over to the fridge and pull out a bottle of water. My body is still on fire. "Carried away?" I ask incredulously. "How the fuck did I even let myself get involved with you!" I screech. Yes, screech. Like a woman possessed.

Rules.

I have plenty of rules, and I break them all the damn time. But this one. I should have never even considered it. He's my dead best friend's widower for fuck sake. If that's not a major screw up, I don't know what is.

"I'll see you on Saturday."

"Oh, you won't be seeing me at all, pal," I toss out. "You're going to leave. You're going to get and not come back."

"I can't do that, Jada."

"Why the hell not, Nicklaus?"

"Because I'm falling for you."

Falling for me?

"That's funny. Men who are falling"—I totally air quote that shit—"for someone don't come over in the middle of the night, give a woman the best orgasm she's had in like forever—if at all ever—and then decide they're moving too fast. Oh, no, men who are 'falling,' finish the fucking job by falling into bed with said woman they are in fact, 'falling' for," I huff out.

"Jada, let me explain."

"You can't. There's nothing to say." I throw my hands up, and as I walk to the trashcan to toss my still full bottle of water out, I say, "Zeus, strike me down with a thunderbolt and put me out of my misery."

There is a grin on Klaus's face. A grin. Why does he think this shit is funny? I don't. His long strides eat up the distance between us, and I'm back in his arms.

"Gorgeous girl. All I'm saying is, I don't want to fuck this up. You're getting bent out of shape for nothing."

That fucking accented voice.

It soothes me.

How is it that one minute he can say something that throws me off the deep end, and the next, I'm putty in his hands. *Sneaky bastard.* My head goes to his chest, and I can hear the crashing of his heart as it plays in my ears. Mine is the same way. He chuckles, and I can feel the vibration in my entire body.

"Amelia told me it would be easy for me to love you," he says against my hair.

"Love me?" I whisper.

"Yeah."

He lifts my head to look up at him.

"I was probably half in love with you a little already. She said you were different. That you weren't like any of her other friends. She talked about how caring you were, and how bent out of shape you would get if things didn't go your way. She also said that when you start to ask Zeus, or any of the other gods of lore for help, that I needed to stop whatever it was I was doing and bring you down from your ledge."

Sounds like Amelia. She always thought I was on the verge of breaking when I asked the gods for help. But I'm not. It's just my coping mechanism. It's a way for me to not overreact.

"I'm not on a ledge. Amelia always thought that, but it isn't the case."

"Really? You weren't about to cut me into a million pieces and bury me in your backyard?"

I snort.

"No, but now that you mention it…it sounds like a grand idea."

He chuckles again.

"I'm sure it does, sunshine. But let's save that for another time."

Before we can finish our conversation, his phone rings. Klaus doesn't let me go but reaches into his pocket to pull out his cell.

"Klaus."

I can't hear who's on the other end, but his arm squeezes me tighter as he listens.

"Yeah, I can be back in about half an hour. Just let me finish wrapping things up with my girl."

*My girl. He called me "his girl."*

And just like that, him stopping things feels like the right thing to do. *For now*, my mind whispers. My body is still upset, but really, should I even be? I had an intense orgasm through stimulation. I know once we get down to the business of breaking in the bed, it's going to be awesome. Be sure when you say "awesome" you have that high-pitched ohm at the end.

"You have to go," I groan.

"Yeah, truck just came in for the night, and the engine is smoking. I'm the only mechanic qualified for engine repairs." Klaus kisses the side of my head. "I'll be back the moment I'm done. You're working tomorrow and then you're off for the weekend?"

"Yeah."

"All right, make dinner for us."

"You don't have that kind of pull, mister," I joke.

"Yeah, I do." He kisses me quickly on the lips and leaves.

What a crazy fucking night.

8

I couldn't sleep most of last night. My body wouldn't let me. It had the kitchen scene between Klaus and me on repeat. I could feel him everywhere. Even places he hadn't yet been or discovered.

When I finally get out of bed, Dali is already waiting for me in the kitchen. I feed her and let her out the back door. Poe is up on the bookcase, surveying all he declares his. But he quickly comes down when he hears me pouring his food.

I need tea. STAT.

I go through my regular routine. I play with Dali and rub Poe's belly. Then shower, dress, and head out the door for work. I see Thomas on my way out, give him a friendly wave, and tell him I am having company for dinner. He waves me off as he sits on his porch and sips his coffee.

I had a lot of time last night to think about everything that took place. The club, the diner, my kitchen. I am hurt by the incident with Caroline, and seriously, I'm shocked she hasn't tried to call me to make amends. But it's only day one, I just need to give her some time. Hell, *I* need time. I haven't really processed that she slept with Jaden, even after knowing how abusive he was towards me. Not to mention crazy.

Dali and I arrive at work and get straight down to training. The dogs in S.E.E.K. are always training. Today, we're working on bomb detection. Dali is a chocolate Lab retriever. She's smart, and graduated at the top of her class. Life without Dali would be boring. That she's my protector, comforter, and all around good listener rolled into one is a bonus. As we run through the drills, my mind keeps drifting back to Klaus. As if sensing my distraction, Dali nudges me with her head and starts making her way through the demo field. She's leash free and basically does her own thing. As her handler, I'm just there to call out the commands or wait for the sign she gives when she's found something.

*Head in the game.*

I have to stop thinking about Klaus.

The barking snaps me out of my daze, and I make my way over to Dali. She's found her target.

"Good girl."

We run through several more drills before lunch. Not too long after that, it's some free time for Dali while I catch up on paperwork before we head home. When I pull up into the drive, I notice Thomas is gone. He must still be hanging out with his cousin. I park the car, grab the groceries, and go about setting things up for dinner while Dali and Poe chill in the backyard.

---

Klaus never said what time he'd be over, and I didn't think to ask. I assume dinner will be around six-thirtyish, seven. But who knows. Being that he works at Dallas Fire and Rescue, there is no telling what time he'll be done. I know today was supposed to be his off day, but one of the trucks had engine trouble. I'm not a mechanic per se. I can do a lot of things most people wouldn't think would interest me, but getting under the hood of a car is sexy to me, and I play around with my own vehicle.

I decide to make stuffed chicken parmesan with a

light marinara sauce and a Greek salad for dinner. For dessert, I stop off at Skye's place to pick up a batch of cupcakes. She is all too excited I'm cooking for Klaus. We chat for about ten minutes before it's time for me to head home to start cooking dinner.

Everything is ready to go, and my dinner turns out perfectly. I even have enough time to shower and toss on a pair of jeans and a tank top. I'm pulling down the plates when I hear a knock at my door. Smiling, I walk out of my kitchen and into the hall to answer it.

Klaus is standing in a one-piece mechanic getup. The top half is down and hanging off his waist, and there is grease everywhere—face, arms, and on his clothes. Correction, he is not Thor's half-brother. Nope. Not even close. I had it wrong this entire time. Did you ever see *Pathfinder* with Karl Urban? No? Then you'd better go and watch that movie. It has it all, including a dark-haired Viking with a body made for sin. Yes, yes, and hell yes, he looks like Ghost from *Pathfinder*, only his hair is up in a messy bun, and his eyes are that fathomless blue with hints of gunmetal grey. He has about three days' worth of scruff on his face, and all that damn grease coating his body highlights all his best features.

"Hey, gorgeous."

Oh, and the voice, I still can't place the accent, but I'm putting my bet on Scandinavian. He has to be cut from Viking cloth. Tonight, we're going to play twenty questions and more.

"Hey, yourself."

"I'd pull you into a hug, but as you can see, I came straight from work."

That's when I notice the overnight bag at his feet.

"You plan on moving in?"

He looks down at the bag.

"No, but I plan to use your shower and change. If that's okay with you."

I nod and let him in, directing him to my guest bathroom.

"Should I be worried about this?" He nods his head in the direction of my bathroom. It's the one decorated in a *Nightmare before Christmas* theme.

"I don't know, should you?"

He looks my way before grinning.

"You're a nut. But I like it."

*You're sexier than hell, and I love it.*

"See you when you get out of the shower."

"Unless you want to join me?" he taunts.

I know he's joking, but I have to remind myself we're taking things slow.

"You couldn't handle what I have to give in the

shower. Remember, slow," I say as I close the door and make a quick exit back to the kitchen. The Viking god in my bathroom is going to be the death of me, and I really hope that before the night is through, he lives up to his ancestor's ways. A girl can always hope for a little midnight marauding.

I'm in the kitchen serving up our plates when Klaus walks in, freshly showered. It's kind of funny because he smells like margaritas. He used my scrub. I grin, and he shakes his head at me, 'cause he knows. He knows he smells like a fruity drink.

"All your soap smells like girly shit."

"Yeah, well, I'm a girl, and I live here," I laugh.

He looks around the kitchen and changes the subject.

"Smells amazing in here."

I can't stop the smile that spreads across my face. I like that he gives compliments freely.

"Great, sit. We're gonna eat, drink, be merry and—"

"Fuck," he interrupts. "We're gonna eat, drink, be merry, and fuck."

I clear my throat. It's the first time he's voiced that particular thought."

"What happen to slow, Klaus?"

He grins.

"Oh, I can fuck you slow, Jada. I can fuck you slow *real* good."

My eyes, if they could, would have rolled all the way back in my head and remained there. This side of Klaus is surprising. He's always been forward, but physically, not verbally. I'm not sure exactly how I feel about this new turn of events. I walk our plates over to the table, and for the next couple of hours we do eat, drink, and talk. When I look up, it's almost one in the morning, and we've polished off two bottles of wine and all of the dessert. We've talked for so long, I practically know everything about him, or at least I think I do. He's from a large family, all of which are still in Iceland, five hours away from Reykjavik. He's a freaking Icelander! I knew it! *Scored me a Viking.* His last name is Aegir. It has something to do with the sea and Norse mythology. His favorite sport is football. He's a Giant's fan, but will tolerate the Raiders. He loves to ride his motorcycle but hates driving in cars. I picked up on that when he took me out last weekend. I don't ask about why, because I already know. The accident.

I tell him all about my family and me. That my parents are divorced but still get along, and that I secretly think they are together but don't want me to know. I tell him about school and how Dali and Poe have been with me forever. We talk about the station and the work I do for S.E.E.K. with the ATF. We go through it all. What we don't talk about are Amelia and his child. I want to, I really do, but I can't push. It's not my place. When he's ready, he'll tell me.

"Can't believe we talked all night," I say, yawning.

"Yeah, never done that before."

"Not even with Amelia?" My eyes go wide, and I can't take the words back. Damn. I didn't want to do the comparison thing, but I couldn't stop the words from coming out of my mouth.

Klaus grins.

"No, not even with Amelia. She wasn't much of a talker. Don't get me wrong, we talked a lot, but we mostly enjoyed each other, life. When I took her back home to Húsavík, she mostly painted, and we took trips. But when we did talk, it was primarily about having a family."

"Do you still want that?"

He lowers his head as if he is thinking for a moment, then looks directly at me before saying. "No, I had that already, Jada. I know what that's all about. Now, I just want to ride my bike, fix cars, and hang out."

Direct.

I can't fault him for that, at least he's honest. But I have to be honest, too.

I am going to bed very angry tonight. There is no doubt in my mind because I am not a 'hang out' type of girl. I do relationships, and I get it, he wants to take things slow, but at the same time, that could mean something different to him than it does to me. I'm not getting any younger, and it isn't that I'm chasing the white picket fence, or even the two-point-five kids. But what I do want is to spend my life with someone, and I can't be bothered with simply 'hanging out.'

"Thanks for your honesty, Klaus."

"I'll always be honest with you, Jada."

Good to know.

I owed him the same.

"Well, I guess since we're being honest, it's my turn to go next. I'm not the person you should be 'hanging out' with. That's not what I'm about. I'm sorry, but we don't want the same things. And I totally understand why you feel the way you feel. But I'm just not built for the kind of relationship you're seeking."

I stand up to clear the plates, and Klaus doesn't stop me. He doesn't say anything either. I don't expect him to. We've basically reached a stalemate. Doesn't matter how attracted we are to one another. It is, what it is. I can't change him, and I'd be foolish to think I can. There are some who would say I could eventually change his mind. But that's not what I want. I want him to want the same things as me; otherwise, it won't be true. Real. I am not going to start a relationship based on a falsehood.

Klaus helps me clean the kitchen, and by the time we're done, it's past two in the morning.

"You can stay here. I don't want you driving this late."

He smirks.

"Sure, I'll stay here."

"Yeah, buddy, don't go there. We're friends, that's it."

Klaus pulls me into his arms so quickly, I barely have time to react. But I do. He looks hurt when I push back and step out of his arms.

"Jada, you have to enjoy life, why not start with me?"

"I do enjoy life, Klaus, very much. I don't deny that I'm attracted to you. I am. You're a hot Viking," I say grinning.

"A Viking, huh?"

There is mischief dancing behind his beautiful eyes, and if I were a weaker woman, I'd totally let him do me in multiple positions, in different parts of the house but I can't. *We don't want the same things.*

"I'll show you to the guest room."

Klaus doesn't say anything else as he follows me. This room is probably the only room in my house that is what most would deem *normal.* There is a queen bed against the wall, cream curtains, and a large oak armoire. I don't follow him inside, I just open the door. As I turn to leave, he grabs both my hands in his and stares down at me.

"Jada, I'm sorry I can't be the things that you want me to be. But I meant what I said."

If that were true, I'd be enough for him to want more than just a hang-out.

"No apology necessary, Klaus. I would never try to change you. It's a good thing we got this all out on the table now and not weeks or months down the road. That would have sucked."

He nods, leans in, and kisses me on the cheek before he goes into the guest room and closes the door.

9

THREE MONTHS LATER

The weekend's here, and Klaus's friends are arriving for yet another get-together. They have been coming over for the last three months, like clockwork. I am having so much fun with everyone; I didn't realize they'd sort of become my family. Since the night we had dinner, Klaus and I texted and even hung out after work. We have all the makings of a real couple, just without the sex and heavy petting. We talk. A lot. We watch a lot of Netflix, minus the chill. Poe and Dali adore him. Klaus is perfect, and as much as I value his friendship, things for me are starting to get serious. But I keep a lid on my feelings. We haven't really known each other long at all, but I am drawn to him. Gravitate in his direction every time he's near.

"Dude, are you seriously going to wear that?" Tammy asks me. The verdict is still out on Hector's old lady. She's cool, but she's also friendly. As in, touchy-feely friendly, in a way that tells me if I were to ever switch sides, she'd be all up on me. Sure she's with Hector, but I get the feeling that she's also into girls, and I'm never wrong about these things.

"Why, what's wrong with what I'm wearing?" I'm in a simple pair of capri pants and a tank top. It's hot as all get out today.

"Nothing, I just thought you'd want to spruce up a bit for Klaus."

"We're just friends, Tammy."

"If you two are friends, then I'm so telling Hector we need to invite you into our circle of *friends*."

See! That proves it right there. I'm never wrong about these things.

"Yeah, not happening. I think you're hot, but that's as far as I'm willing to go."

"Yeah, I know, but still… You and Klaus are definitely not 'friends.' Chops' little brother, Koda, is out there, and he's been checking out your ass. Klaus almost killed him."

Really?

"He's just being protective."

"Whatever, Jada. Act like you don't notice the way

he looks at you, and I'll act like I don't notice the way you swoon over him."

I look at Tammy from across the kitchen island and groan. I have to talk to someone. Caroline and I haven't spoken since the night back at the club. Not that I plan to speak to her, but she was my only female friend. Now, I have Tammy, Chops' lady, Sabina, and the other girls that hang out with Klaus and his friends.

"Tammy, we're just friends. Seriously. Klaus and I don't want the same things."

"That's what he thinks. He wants it bad, he's just too chickenshit to act on it. Trust me, go out there and flirt with Koda, and I guarantee you'll see another side of Klaus."

"Doubtful. But I'm not one to play games."

"Everyone has a game, Jada. Whether we want to admit it or not. You're just too blind to see you've already put in your hand."

I don't respond; instead, I tell her to help with all the side dishes. There have to be at least forty people on my property today, and I'm actually okay with that. Thomas has been grumpy ever since Klaus and I started hanging out together. He even gave notice a few weeks back so the cottage next to the house is empty. Although I miss Thomas's help, the empty cottage has come in handy. Especially when people drink a little too much. The second barbeque I had, more than half of them were camped out in my house and in the guest room. It was not a pretty sight.

As I head out the front door, Koda is there, grabbing one of the bowls from my hand.

"Hey, let me help you with that."

"Thanks."

Koda looks like Chops, only a younger, hotter version. He has dark, chestnut-brown hair with gold highlights, and he keeps it messy but in a way that still comes off as sexy, and his eyes are the color of maple syrup. Not too dark and not too light, but warm with golden highlights. A girl would be crazy not to want him, but my stupid body only wants one person. He just happens to be unavailable for the kind of relationship I want.

*Just give in and hang out.* That's my body talking. My mind, on the other hand, is telling me to stay true to my course. I'm not getting any younger, and I know in order to find the *one,* you have to put yourself out there. I get it. I'm not opposed to getting out there, what I am opposed to, is getting out there and finding out where I'm getting will lead to nowhere.

When I set the stuff down on the table, Koda reaches out and takes my elbow gently.

"How come we've never gone out?" he asks.

I'm a bit shocked, and don't know how to respond, but I don't even get the chance.

I've read in books where the heroine can sense her hero, and I kid you not, the moment Klaus is standing behind me, I can feel the heat of his stare on my neck. But it's not a warm stare, it's cold, as in angry. He's pissed.

"Jada isn't for you," is all Klaus rumbles. Then I feel the actual heat of him at my back, not just his glare.

"Klaus," I say in warning.

"Seriously, Klaus. You haven't made a move on her, and I figure you won't. We all get it, man. You're unavailable. But you don't own, nor do you have a claim on Jada. You're not her keeper."

"She's mine," he mumbles.

Did I just hear that right?

I can't be sure, but I could have sworn I just heard Klaus say I was his? What the hell is that about?"

"All right, you two, to make this not a big deal, I'll just go on record as saying that I'm not for either of you. All right? We're here to eat, drink, and be merry. I don't want *Clash of the Titans* going down in my yard."

"I'd pay to see that!" Hector yells over towards the three of us.

"It wouldn't even be a clash, more like a one-two, goodnight," Chops says. He walks over and cuffs Koda on the back of the head before heading back over to the barbeque grill.

Both men are staring each other down, and I'm reluctant to leave. I really don't want them fighting. It's unnecessary.

---

The shenanigans from this afternoon's display of male testosterone have dissipated. I'm sitting on the back porch, sipping my Crispin Pear, when Koda sits on the bottom step and looks up at me.

"Jada, can I ask you something?"

"Shoot."

"What happened back there was childish." Koda rubs the back of his neck and looks up at me sideways. "I don't usually get that way over a female. But you're beautiful and funny. I know it's like unspoken lore around here that you and Klaus will end up together, but seriously, why not hang out with me?"

Seriously? Was that the going rate for my time? Hanging out? I look over at Koda, then take another sip of my drink. Klaus has avoided me most of the day, and it's not like him.

"Koda, I don't want you to get the wrong idea, but hanging out with me is the equivalent of us just being friends. If you're okay with that, I'm okay with that. But nothing more. Got it?"

His eyes narrow slightly, and he turns to look at everyone out in the yard. Dali is running around playing catch with Hector while Tammy cheers them on. Poe is on the railing, watching. Chops is cleaning my grill, and Klaus is… *Holy shit.* I spot Klaus off in the distance, and he's basically all hugged up on Breeze. There is a reason everyone calls her Breeze. She's easy. Like a breeze, she goes wherever her damn crotch takes her. Honestly, I can't even tell you how I'd normally react, but it's nothing like I'm used to acting. Before I know it, I'm up and out of my chair and stomping my way across the yard to both of them.

Klaus's head turns in my direction, and he literally looks at me as if I'm an afterthought. Like we haven't been spending time together. Yeah, we're friends, but we're also friends who seriously want to get down to business. We just don't act on it. *Did you truly expect him to get his head out of his ass?* I know I don't hold a claim to him, but what he's doing right now, in my yard, is disrespectful.

"Jada, what's up?"

*Oh, now he's mister casual.*

"What's up? Really? That's all you got?"

Klaus has the nerve to look at me as if I'm the one who's lost their marbles.

"Hey, Jada, do you think Klaus and I can stay in the cottage tonight?" Breeze purrs. Her arms tighten around Klaus, and I swear I see nothing but her death. Repeatedly. It's like an ongoing loop in my head as Quincy Jones' *Ironside*, from *Kill Bill Vol. 1*, plays in my mind. I don't see red, I think, *"Kill Breeze."* My jealousy burns with murderous intent, and I can't do anything but grin as I say, "No, the cottage is being renovated."

"It is?" Breeze asks. She's clearly disappointed. But Klaus knows I'm lying. He also knows why.

"Klaus, can I talk to you for a moment?"

He untangles himself from Breeze, who isn't at all happy.

I could care less.

I start walking. I don't have to look back to see if

he's following. I know he is. I walk inside the house. No one's inside. I hear the sliding glass door click after Klaus enters. That's when I turn.

"What the hell is wrong with you?"

"Nothing, Jada. We're friends."

"Friends."

"Friends," he repeats slowly.

"So I mean nothing to you? You said you were half in love with me."

His eyes darken for a moment before they clear.

"I know what I said."

"So why are you all hugged up on Breeze? Seriously, Breeze?"

"I already told you, I just want to hang out. I'm not going to invest my time in another relationship. I'm a man, and if you're not going to hang out, then, it is what it is."

That was way harsh.

That's when I lose it.

"Invest your time? You're a man!?" I scream. "You're already invested. You spend almost every day with me when you're not at the station. You've spent the night. We've even fallen asleep together, my head in your lap. How much investment is left after that? Whether you want to admit it or not, we're in a relationship." It's like a light bulb goes off after I define us. "You almost threw down with Koda out there, and all he wanted to do was help me carry shit out to the table."

Klaus grunts.

"Jada, we're friends. That's it. It's about time we start acting appropriately. Hanging out with you has obviously given you a false image of us." His eyes are stern. His voice is deep without even a hint of emotion. Nothing. It's as if he's shut down.

"What's happened between yesterday and today?"

He shrugs as if nothing is out of the ordinary.

"I don't want to lead you on, and that's what I've been doing. I'm not the man for you, Jada, and you're not Amelia."

My chest caves in as I try to pull air into my lungs. I don't move. I can't. But Klaus does. He delivers the death blow and walks away. I don't see him leave, but I hear the pipes from his motorcycle. I'm sick to my stomach because I really thought he'd eventually realize that what we were doing was creating the foundation for *us*. I misread that one like an idiot. I didn't realize it either, not until Tammy pointed out that he was chickenshit. And he is. He's a big fat pile of chickenshit.

Fuck.

I'm crying.

Again.

Me, crying, is never a good thing. Like ever. Because things get bad, and, I'm a horrible crier. It's like Pai-Mei's five-finger exploding chest act. Silent at first, then I just break down until I almost die. Yes, I'm still on the whole *Kill Bill* streak because let's face it, my situation is perfect for it. Did Klaus just shoot me in the fucking head and leave me to die?

Fuck yes.

Is *A silhouette of Doom* by Ennio Morricone playing loudly in my head as I plot the untimely death of Breeze? It's like I'm Norman Bates and Beatrix Kiddo all wrapped into one. Because I really want to cut a bitch with my Hattori Hanzo sword. *For fucking real!* And I hope I catch her in the shower when I do it.

*Calm.*

*Deep.*

*Breaths.*

*Jada.*

"Oh, honey, your face." My head darts over in Tammy's direction. She looks at me with pity, and that's when I almost lose hold of the reins keeping me together.

"Tammy, I'm not feeling very well. Can you tell everyone they need to leave?"

"Are you sure, honey?"

I frantically nod my head as I make my way into the house to my bedroom and close the door. My body slides down to the floor in a slump against the wood. The tears come quickly and freely now. My nose starts to drip until I slide to the side and lay my face on the floor and just cry. I don't know if anyone can hear me, and frankly, I don't care. How could he just toss us to the side like that? Why would he tell me that I'm not Amelia? I know that! I fucking told him this was a bad idea from the beginning, but still, he insisted. Then, when things got to be too much, he put on the brakes, only to fall back on the *friend card.* Even then, we both knew we were lying to one another. I could see it in his face. In his actions. What he was doing didn't scream "friend." It said we were more than that. My feelings were out in the universe, and I knew he'd caught them. Hell, it was obvious, just like Tammy said. I'd done more than swoon for the idiot. Friends didn't stare at each other with warm eyes and let the look linger. Friends didn't hold hands while they were grocery shopping or fall asleep cuddled on the couch. Okay, maybe they did cuddle on the couch, but in all the history of friendom, when did it become okay to rip another's heart from their chest and leave it beating at their feet? Um, never. Yet, here I lie, on my floor, crying like a damn baby. I don't know how long I'm there, but Dali is at the door, whining. I know she's worried about me. I'm sure Poe is, too, in his own weird way, but I can't move. Not right now. I don't want to.

Just can't.

I'm in my own personal hell. Constructed and locked by me.

My mind goes over everything. I analyze things from beginning to end, looking for signs. Something that will tell me that I was either right on the money or way off my mark. But there's not one single event that would deny what we had was more than friendship. We'd spent so much time together, and maybe that was the *thing* I should have looked deeper into. Maybe I was the delusional one. Hell, I talk to my dog and cat. My house looks like a tween had a field day with the décor.

*He didn't take you or your time seriously,* my mind supplies, and I'm crying again. I cry for so long and so hard that I finally drift off.

10

90 DAYS POST KLAUS...

It's been exactly three months sans Klaus. Three. Things eventually got better. It still hurts to think about him, but I am doing my best to put it all behind me. The barbeques stopped after that day, and although I see Tammy and Hector on occasion, they both know Klaus is off limits as far as conversation topics go. Every once in a while, Chops and Sabina will stop by and chat with me. But no one ever mentions Klaus. I'm thankful.

I've been avoiding the station like the plague. I don't want to see him. Can't be around him yet. I know what my limits are, and seeing Klaus again is a huge no-no. I threw myself into work, taking on jobs that are way outside of Dallas in some cases. Even thought of moving but decided that I love my little farm too much.

Today has been particularly hard for me, and it isn't even Klaus-related. There have been several more fires. This one is particularly nasty. A couple of the guys from the station respond to the call and Kenneth and Jules get busy securing the family. After the rescue, Dali and I were on the scene.

When they pulled the little, three-year-old girl, Emma, from the fire, she was unconscious and barely breathing. Severely burned. My heart goes out to her and her family. I watch as the mother sobs into her husband's chest. My heart is shattered. I agonize over all the different things I know must be going through the mother's and father's minds. Dali stays by their side, and it isn't until the mother comes up to thank me for allowing Dali to hang out with them that I break down. I don't think Klaus is the cause, but as I stand there with tears running down my face, I realize that he *is* the reason. He may not have lost his family in a fire, but he did lose his family. Both parents are devastated at the idea that their daughter may not survive. It's like I can feel what they're feeling, and I know right then that if and when I choose to love that deeply, I'll be rocked to my core. Shaken in such a way that I know the damage will be irreparable.

How can anyone be prepared to lose the people they love? Especially given that the amount of time they have together is so short. Who can put a timeframe on someone's heart? No one can tell me when my grieving should be over; it's up to me to decide. It will be up to Klaus to decide when he's ready to move on from the loss of his family. I won't be the deciding factor, he will. I hug the mother quickly and tell her how great Kenneth and Jules are. Her head bobs up and down vigorously.

"Thank you again for allowing your dog to sit with us."

"No problem. She's really good at calming people."

Dali is sitting next to me as I watch the parents walk to the ambulance where their daughter is being treated. That's when I see Kenneth walking toward me.

"Why haven't we seen you down at the station?"

"Been really busy, Kenneth."

"Too busy to visit your friends?"

*If only that were the real reason.*

I can't tell him about Klaus and me. I'm just not ready to have that conversation, and Kenneth and I don't have that type of friendship. It's more of co-worker with some brotherly affection than anything else. We never get into the heavier side of feelings. It just isn't our thing.

"I'll try and stop by when you have your next cookout."

"Girl, we are always cooking. This weekend, we're doing a pancake breakfast for one of our many charities."

Damn.

I love pancakes.

"I'll see what I can do. Send the information to my cell. I gotta get going. Dali needs a bath after today."

"All right, I'll see you this weekend, Jada."

"Sure thing, Kenneth."

But I know I'm not going. I can't. Klaus will be there.

The pancake breakfast comes and goes without incident. I don't show. I do text Kenneth to tell him that something came up. He accepts my lie for what it is, and I think I'm in the clear. It's Saturday afternoon when everything literally blows up in my face.

Grocery shopping. I hate every single damn minute of grocery shopping. Can't I order my shit online? Sure, but I tried that once and ended up with stale bread, brown lettuce, and milk that was at least four days old. I would like to think myself practical, but I know I'm not. I'm quirky. I say what's on my mind, and I basically make no damn sense when I'm flustered. Hell, I quote movies when I get nervous and at the most inopportune times. I hear music in my head. It's like I walk around with a multitude of theme songs. But my animals love me, and I have a job that I enjoy. As far as I'm concerned, I'm a full-fledged functioning adult.

I'm in the cereal aisle when I hear giggling on the other side. Nothing out of the ordinary. Not really. It's just some chick having a good laugh. Her laugh is actually infectious, and if I were in the same aisle as she was, I know we'd make eye contact and share a chuckle. Only she'd be the only one privy to what's so funny.

"I love you so much, Klaus."

I freeze at the use of *his* name. Then I wait. I can't move. Can't breathe. I need to hear if it's *my* Klaus. *He was never yours.* True. I know this, don't need to be reminded, but when the voice finally does respond, my heart implodes in on itself, then explodes into an infinite amount of shards until there is nothing left but a deflated organ.

"Is that so?" It's him. That smooth, accented voice that rumbles along my spine and destroys what's left of my sanity. How did he come to mean so much to me? Why is it that a man I barely know affects me so much? I know the answer to those questions. I do know him, inside and out. He'd become my best friend. There was a level of attraction so deep and so strong that it was a miracle we were able to tamp it down. But now he's with someone else. Another woman has fallen under his spell and his charm and those brilliant eyes. Eyes that cast shadows but reflect kindness. Eyes, that, when he looked at me, all I could see was myself reflected back in them. I need my head checked. I need to get out of this damn aisle before I'm found out. But the woman's question stops my retreat.

"Yeah. How come you never say it back?" the female voice asks.

I'm straining to hear his response. I'm wishing we were in one of those stores where if you moved the cereal box to the side, you'd get a sneak peek at what's going on in the other aisle.

"Breeze, you know I don't do relationships. Not with anyone."

Ugh.

Breeze.

I'd like to tell you *Kill Bill* did not sound in my head again, but it does. It's louder, possibly even stronger than before, but I try and ignore it.

"You say that, but I'm at your place almost every night warming your bed."

I gasp.

And yeah, it's loud. Like so loud, I know they heard me. Like a coward, I leave my cart and book it over three more aisles before I feel safe. I should leave. But I don't. It's not because I'm a glutton for punishment. It's because my cart is still there, and my purse is in the damn thing. Fuck my life!

Oh, and the little old lady that was in the aisle with me, she literally chases me down in her go-cart.

"Ma'am. Ma'am."

I turn in her direction.

"Yes?"

"You left your purse in your shopping cart. I would have brought it to you, but I can't stand too good on my own."

I try and play it off like it's no big deal. When it is. *Can't leave the store without your purse, which contains your keys, dumbass.*

Duh. I know this.

"Thanks, I was actually looking for something, I forgot about. Thank you."

"You young people really need to remember things. I'm going to be eighty-two on Thursday, and even I remember not to leave my purse." The old lady shakes her head as she drives away. Guess she put me in my place. My insides are queasy as I slowly walk back to where I left my shopping cart. It's there. Right where I left it, but so is Klaus. He still looks the same —tall, dark brown hair pulled back in a bun, barely shaved face, and those eyes…those remarkable ice-blue eyes with hints of grey. They see right through me.

"Jada," he whispers my name like a prayer, and I take a huge step back. I don't want to face this. I don't want any part of what he has to say. Not right now. The wound that has been slowly healing due to my revelation has opened back up. I knew it would happen. I knew he'd find someone else and that it would be in stages, but somehow, I always thought he'd go through the stages with me.

"Klaus."

I notice Breeze isn't with him. He must have told her to go on and finish shopping. They were shopping together. *Together.* Like a normal couple. We'd gone shopping together. *Stop it, Jada. Stop it right there.* I can't over analyze; I'll drive myself crazy.

"How've you been?"

"Great." I lie. "You?"

"I miss you," he rumbles.

Whoa. That was not what I expected to come out of his mouth. I was thinking it would be the same as me, just a "good," or a "great." Not an "I miss you." How could I have been so off the mark on that one? Better yet, how do I respond?

"Wasn't expecting to hear you say that."

"Why not?"

I shrug.

"Why would I?"

"We spent almost every fucking day together. Of course, I miss you."

"Well, now you have Breeze." The words are out before I can stop them, and I know it's petty.

"I don't have Breeze. We just spend time together."

That is total code for, "we just fuck."

"Okay, you spend time together, but you don't need me around for that." I try and walk past him to get to my cart, but Klaus catches me around the waist and pulls my back to his front. I can feel the heat of his hand through my shirt as it spans the length of my stomach. The hard press of his body as he holds me tighter almost does me in. All I want to do is die and melt at the same time. But I'm not going to read anything into this. I can't. His breath is coming fast and hot against my cheek as he speaks into my ear.

"I'm sorry if I hurt you, Jada."

"I'm fine, Klaus."

"Then how come you haven't come by the station? The guys have noticed. Kenneth keeps asking me how you're doing," he growls as his arm pulls me tighter.

"I've been busy, Klaus, and to be honest, I can't… not knowing how I feel about you. About us. Don't worry, I get it. I understand. You lost your family. They can never be replaced. But I wasn't trying to replace Amelia or your son. I was just hoping there was enough room in there for me and the love I had to offer."

I just said that.

Oh my God.

I just said that.

Out loud.

I might as well have quoted *Notting Hill*. You know the infamous line, *"I'm just a girl."* Yeah, so not cool on so many levels, as the male lead basically shuts her down. Swats her hopes down like a freaking fly.

I'm waiting for the other shoe to drop, for the bomb to hit, but no words come from Klaus. His breathing is still erratic. His hand is applying pressure to my stomach, and as a result, my will is breaking. *He's here with someone else.* Right. Breeze.

"Please, let me go."

"Let you go?" he says it as if he's confused. Or maybe he realizes we both need to let go. I need to let go of him and soon. One day soon, he's going to have to let go of the notion that his life is on stand-by.

His arm releases me, and I quietly make my way over to my shopping cart. I know he's still standing there, staring. But I can't be bothered to look. I won't look. Instead, I raise my hand up and wave as I say, "Goodbye, Nicklaus."

## 11

### 184 DAYS LATER AFTER TOTAL ANNIHILATION

The incident in the grocery store was six months ago. Six whole months. But I'm better now. Things started to fall into place for me the moment I realized a few things about myself. One, I had been stuck in a rut of sorts, too. Since Jaden, I'd become a bit of a cynic. I used my job and my animals to disconnect from the world around me. I didn't have a bad life, but it was far from perfect. I thought I had my heart broken by Caroline and Jaden, but really, it was nothing compared to what I felt after realizing Klaus was no longer going to be a part of my life. There was a sort of epiphany at the grocery store that day. I'd said what I'd been too afraid to voice even to myself. I loved him, and I was really hoping to have space in his heart. I didn't want it all, I knew a huge part of it belonged to Amelia and his son; and at first, I was against the whole thought of us exploring the possibilities. Amelia would want him happy, and I thought I could be the one to give him that happiness.

But how does one explore, when we never got the chance. A few heated kisses and an almost close encounter hardly counts. But it was everything after that, that did. The time spent getting to know one another. The phone calls and time spent with friends who are now my friends. We fell into a relationship-like pattern. There were things missing, like sex, but we cooked for one another. Watched movies, and were *us*. The best part about the entire situation was that even though he never said it, and probably didn't know he was showing it, Klaus loved me in his own way. As I loved him. Maybe it wasn't a romantic kind of love, but it was definitely love, and I felt it. It was real. Tangible. Something that if nurtured and watered would have grown into an amazing kind of love.

Hector and Tammy are getting married, and Chops and his girl had a little boy, who everyone affectionately calls Chops Jr.. Koda has moved into the cottage house as my new farmhand and is doing a wonderful job. He needed the money, and actually knows a lot about farming. I've made it clear to Koda that the only hand I need is on the farm itself. Dating and flirting is off limits. Dali and Poe even like his company, so all is right in the world. I'm even throwing another barbeque.

Tammy is staring at me as I pull my braids into a ponytail on top of my head.

"Explain to me again what protective style means and how the hell is it crocheted into your real hair?"

She's talking about my braids. Summer is right around the corner, and I'm trying to grow my hair back out. I've kept it short for so long I thought it was time for a change. I explain the process to her, even show her where the braids and my hair connect. When she finally gets it, she smiles.

"How long does it take?"

"About three hours, sometimes more depending on who's doing my hair, but Kianna is the best at what she does."

"Well, you look great."

"Thanks."

The loud roar of bikes and trucks can be heard pulling up into the drive, and I turn to Tammy and pull her in close.

"Glad you made me do this."

She laughs.

"It's time. Everyone misses your smiling face, and your place is ideal. You have enough land, and, well, you could say we're all using you for the space on your property."

"Right. You all are just here because I make a mean pecan pie."

"That, too."

All the food is prepped, and the grill has been going for the last hour. Tammy and I gather in the kitchen where Sabina is rinsing off Chop Jr.'s pacifier.

"I swear that boy has his daddy's ways."

"Well, we can't all be as good-looking as me," Chops says, walking into the kitchen. "Meat's on the grill and, Jada girl, you have company."

"I should hope so."

Chops shakes his head.

He stopped calling me "girl," after Jr. was born. Now, I've graduated to "Jada girl."

"No, not us, honey. Him." Sabina points in the direction of the hall, and I look and see Klaus standing there. My first reaction is absolute stunned silence. Nothing moves. Nothing exists. Everyone disappears and it's just us. *Dammit.* He's in dark, distressed jeans, and a black tee that's stretched tightly over his arms and abs. He cut his hair, but not too much, there is still a lot of it there, wavy and worthy of a finger comb. His eyes don't look blue at the moment, but rather a steely grey. There is new ink on his arm, and I can't really tell what it is but it's something tribal.

He still has a hold of me, and here I thought I was doing so much better.

There are a slew of things going through my brain, and I kid you not, I'm filtering out the top twenty-five most romantic lines ever said on-screen. Well, top twenty-five to me. I'm going through them fast and wondering which line will be his. Does he even have a line? Is he trying to reconnect? Maybe he just wants to be friends? *Yup, he's here to tell you, you've been friend-zoned indefinitely.* Anything is possible at the moment. What I should be doing is trying to figure out what I'm going to say to him in response to whatever he says to me. *No. That's wrong.*

I can't be thinking of a response. I need to give him my undivided attention. That is one of the first things when it comes to listening and communicating.

Undivided attention.

Remove distractions. Which means our audience in the kitchen needs to leave. I need to focus and stay focused, and I need to make sure I let him get what he needs to say out before I say what I want to say—if anything at all.

"Could you guys give us a moment?" I ask. *Remove the distractions.*

Klaus seems relieved I didn't ask him to leave. I'm a bit surprised, too. I'm not hurt; there is no reason to be hurting at this point. I understand why he is the way he is. He hasn't moved on yet, and until that happens fully, he will always be who he is now. A man trapped in the past. Everyone leaves but not before Chops gives Klaus a pat on the shoulder and walks out.

"Do you want something to drink?"

"No, just want to talk to you."

"Okay."

He doesn't say anything, but neither do I. I'm trying to be a good listener. Even if it takes him a moment to articulate what it is he wants to say. He motions for us to sit on the couch in my living room. I follow him and I feel like this is where he sits on one end of the couch and I on the other. But that's not what happens at all. I take the corner, and he's right there next to me. Our legs are touching, our shoulders brush, and he turns so he's seated at an angle and grabs both my hands.

"When you told me to let you go in the store that

day, it shocked me. It shocked me because you were right. I hadn't let go of you, and that made me realize that somehow, I'd gotten ahold of you. I didn't lie when I said I was halfway in love with you. Whether you want to say you were under my skin or already inside my heart doesn't matter. You where there. I thought I could handle casual with you. I didn't seek you out because my wife told me to. Hell, I didn't even try to. But there you were in Sulphur, looking cute and sexy, and the moment I saw you, I knew you. Then, when we reconnected, things started to move faster than I expected. It felt like you were taking me further and further away from their memory. So I did what I thought I had to do to protect myself from that.

"I know I hurt you in the process, and that wasn't my intention. I was selfish because I was only looking out for me and my interests. Even though I tried to get you out of my heart, I can't. You're there, and so are they. Amelia is there, Nico is there, and you, sweet Jada, are there, too. Taking up the dark space void of light and filling it with love. I broke things off with Breeze that day. And every day since then, I've been trying to get the courage to come over here and knock on your door. Get back what's mine. I don't want to let you go. Not now or ever."

That was way better than I expected or could have hoped for. But I don't get a chance to really voice my opinion. Klaus, in his infinite Viking mandom, has decided that he's going to take control of the conversation a different way. He doesn't even ask. Just takes. His mouth closes over mine in a bruising kiss. It's long, deep, but he somehow manages to make it soft and slow at the same time. I'm overwhelmed with joy. I know I'm going to be feeling this kiss for days.

Between kisses he says, "Please tell me we can try this again."

"You mean be friends?" I'm smiling against his lips.

"No, smartass. Friends don't kiss like this," he growls into my lips, then proceeds to show me, how not-friends we're going to be.

I pull back and look him in the eyes. There is so much emotion there. Warmth, love, and all kinds of amazing. I'm speechless.

"You sure this time?"

"Yeah, gorgeous, I'm more than sure."

---

We end up in my room, and I can hear the laughter outside as the others talk and eat.

But the moment Klaus's lips are on my neck, the sounds fade away. My body is humming with pent-up lust. I'm feeling too much all at once, and we haven't even gotten to the good parts yet. Klaus's hands are everywhere. My neck, my chest, my arms, legs, stomach. There isn't a place they haven't travelled, and I can't help but feel taken. My body is plastered up against the wall as he drops to his knees. I can't help it, my excitement has me skittish, and my chest is starting to burn from lack of air. The palms of his hands are hot to the touch as they skim up my bare legs. I'm glad I went with a maxi dress and lacey underwear.

"I don't think I can be gentle this first time," Klaus says against the inside of my thigh, right before he bites down. My eyes roll back in my head because I can't focus. My body has become his personal playground, and I'm the kid at the front of the line anxiously waiting my turn. His hands shove my dress up and around my hips, where he holds the material tightly as he buries his head between my legs. His mouth tugs on my panties, and I'm a bit shocked at his actions. I kid you not, although my mind is clouded with lust, my brain has not forgotten about things that could possibly go wrong when a man has his head buried between your legs. But just as the thought hits me, Klaus gathers the ends of my dress in one hand and uses the other to pull my underwear down to fall at my ankles. He pulls in several deep breaths as if he can't get enough of my scent. My body wants him to rush forward, and my mind is shutting down. All sane thoughts have flown out the window.

He doesn't devour me right away. No, he prolongs it, drags the moment out until I'm literally panting, and my legs are about to turn to jelly. His hot breath fans over my heated core, and as he takes in a deep breath, he lets out a low hum of appreciation.

"You smell like peaches and sugar."

*Thank you, peach sugar scrub.*

"And you're wet."

His finger dips into my center and comes back glistening with my juices. I watch as he sucks my juices off his finger, my heart beating frantically as my chest heaves. *Damn, that's hot.* I don't know what sets him off, or how things go from torturous teasing to death by devouring, but his mouth quickly replaces his fingers and begins to do amazing things, causing me to see stars; although, me hitting my head against the wall repeatedly might have something to do with that. He's kissing me down there, and it's a different kind of kiss. A sensory overload that takes hold of my body from the inside out. Right when I'm about to fall over, my legs are lifted, and the other hand at my waist disappears, which causes my dress to fall on top of Klaus's head. It doesn't stop his actions. My legs are tossed over his shoulders, and he goes from being on his knees to standing up. My pussy still attached to his mouth as he licks and sucks and latches on to my clit. The sound of him eating me out is something I will never forget. It's loud and animalistic. His appetite is voracious. Seconds turn into minutes, and as the minutes pass, my body heat is soaring higher and higher until my stomach pitches and my core tingles with that telltale sign of my impending orgasm. Only it's coming down on me way too fast. Like a speeding bullet, it shoots straight to my core and imbeds itself in its intended target. Me.

The sound that comes from my mouth isn't one I've heard before. Like, ever. It's a cross between a cry and a moan that stretches on for so long and so loud that I know the others outside sitting on the porch know what's happening in here. But I don't get a chance to bounce back. Klaus has positioned me in such a way that I slide down his chest. I'm still against the wall, but it's like I'm slowly being moved, almost floating. I feel the button of his jeans on the back of my thighs, and I wonder when—and how—

he got his jeans open so fast. But that's not what has my eyes wide like saucers. Nope, not in the least. It's the size of his condom-covered cock. This isn't my first ride, and I know a good size penis when I feel one. But, damn. The size and girth were obviously bestowed upon him by the gods who await him in Valhalla.

"My Viking," I murmur against his lips.

Klaus smiles. Our eyes are locked, and I can see the feral intent in his gaze. He said he couldn't be gentle this first time around, yet he's trying to read if I'm ready. Another reason to love him. Even when he really wants to be harsh with me, he still finds the time to be patient.

"I'm ready," I whisper and kiss him deeply, tasting myself on his lips as his hands tighten around my waist.

He stretches me slowly as he lowers me onto his length. I'm so wet, so aroused, it takes no time at all for me to get adjusted. When I'm fully seated, he uses his hands to lift me up. I try to see what we look like joined but can't. My dress is in the way, and he's still in his jeans. We're fucking with our clothes on, and in a way, it's sexy. We're clothed, concealing ourselves from what it is our bodies are doing to one another, yet I can feel everything. Every thrust, every pull, and every breath. I feel it all. I may not be able to see our connection, but fuck, can I feel it.

The rhythm Klaus sets is brutal. The wall is the only thing keeping me up at this point. Frames are falling. The constant pounding and thumping is both a rhythm and a reminder of just how bruised my back is going to be when this is all over. But I can't bring myself to care. The sounds of my moans and his grunts join the chorus as our bodies continue to crash into one another.

"Fuck, I love your pussy. It's magic," Klaus murmurs into the side of my neck. "Come on my cock, gorgeous, I need you to, I'm not going to last much longer."

My mind blanks, and my body seizes from his words alone. He wedges as hand between us and grips the base of his cock, and for a moment, I'm not sure what's happening. His fingers are wet as they trail across the cheek of my ass, and before I can even fathom what happens next, I feel the invasion. My mind goes blank and my mouth opens on a silent scream. The dual sensation has my body shifting and my hips twisting as I grind down on his cock. And just when I think I can't hold on any longer, a surge of energy bursts through me, ripping me apart, as I careen forward into a pit of bliss-filled ecstasy.

Klaus grinds up into me over and over, prolonging my orgasm until finally, he lets out a muffled roar against my shoulder. I short circuit, and my sight dims until I see a bright burst of colors. I feel his teeth sink into my neck, and my body seizes again as mini orgasms leave me sated and exhausted.

"Damn." It's all I can say as my body sags.

"I don't think I can move," he says against my skin, placing tiny kisses along my neck and shoulder.

"Well, we can't stay like this all day," I tease.

"Why not?"

"I have guests."

"They can wait."

Klaus carries me over to the bed. He leaves me to dispose of the condom. We're both still in our clothes, only the buttons of his jeans are undone, and I can tell he's not wearing his shoes any longer. He climbs up on my bed and stretches out next to me.

"So, you think I'm a Viking?" he says conversationally.

"Yeah, my Viking," I say without shame.

His laugh is deep and pleasant. We both turn to look at each other and just stare. I don't know what he's thinking, and I don't even pretend to guess. But I know what *I'm* thinking. Nicklaus and I are beginning something new. What? I'm not sure, but it's something long-lasting. I can't predict the future, or even guestimate how much time we have. I don't want to.

I'm not going to plan this one out. I'm leaving it to chance.

Life is too short to worry about the *what if's*. I need to be concerned with what's happening right now, and right now, I'm happy. Completely happy.

EPILOGUE

DALI

I look on as the male stares at his female human. *My* human. It took them a long time to figure things out. I will never understand why humans make it so hard to just do what needs to be done. Poe's the one who figured out that the male, who calls himself Nicklaus, is the same male that the human Amelia kept talking about.

Amelia and her small human are now at peace. At least, that's how Poe describes it. He says he's the only one who can see, being as he's the smarter of us. His words. I let him think that's true, but it's not. The fact that my kitty brother hasn't mastered getting baths from our human is beyond me. Instead, the cat prefers to lick himself. He also likes to just sit and watch. Everything. I don't watch, I interact. So if the cat wants to think he's smart, who am I to deny him? Everyone knows dogs are the dominant species. I have a job, and a job I enjoy, and it gets me lots of treats and recognition. Not to mention the belly rubs and baths. Oh, yes, baths are one of my favorite pastimes. I am a Lab, after all. Water is kind of my thing.

Poe is sitting on the counter while the male human makes his bowl of disgusting-smelling cat food. I have already been fed by my human and am content enough to keep watch on the male. I like Nicklaus. He takes great care of my momma, Jada. He doesn't make her cry, never says a harsh word to her. There was that one time, though, when they were sharing words with one another about getting a bigger car for the baby that was soon to be coming into the world.

I plop down on the floor, my belly hitting the cool tile in the kitchen. We're adding to our family. The two humans don't know what they're having, but Poe and I do. Amelia all but squealed in delight when she found out the two humans were breeding.

*"Keep a close eye on them, Dali. Make sure they do everything in their power to cherish their little one. And, Poe, you be sure to watch over the baby and help Dali out when she needs it. I have a feeling this little guy is going to be more of a handful than my little Nico."*

All I could think was, *Great. They're having one of those kinds of babies.* I was always the center of attention, and when Poe came along, he was so independent, he didn't require the type of care I do. So there was never a threat, but now, there's a baby human coming. Baby humans are needy.

"All right, Poe, eat up. No bothering Jada this morning. Let me do all the heavy lifting, and you just stay there and be the cat I know you to be."

Klaus will only hear Poe's meow, as just that—a meow. But what Poe really says is that the male human has nothing to worry about. Because today is the day the little human is coming. I whine. Momma's short breaths have alerted me. It's time. The new baby is coming, and although I'm not too keen on being left behind, I know I'll wait to pass judgment on the new human when we have a chance to meet. But for now, I need to alert Klaus of the situation. I let out a loud bark and stand, getting Klaus's attention. I walk over and butt my head against Momma's thigh.

"Hey there, Dali, it's almost time to meet your new family member."

"It's time? Already?" Klaus asks. I look between both humans, and like always, Momma knows exactly what I'm thinking.

"Yes, Dali, Klaus is just a little flustered."

Someone called a mid-wife is on standby, and Klaus pulls the object from his pocket that allows humans to speak back and forth over long distances.

"It's time, Clare, how soon can you be here? Right? Hot water, soak in the tub, ETA, ten minutes."

I don't have a concept of time, only when it comes to the time between my feedings. Life is simple for me. But it seems as if things happen fast.

Klaus moves to scoop Momma Jada up in his arms, and they disappear into the back of the house. Soon after that, the human called a mid-wife shows up, and moments later, a loud crying is heard. I'm not used to the sound, but it makes me anxious. And I don't like that. What are they doing in there? I run to the back of the house, and Poe follows behind as we make it to the closed door. I bark and scratch at the door until it's finally opened.

The room smells different.

Someone new.

Someone theirs. *Ours.*

I walk over to the side of the bed. Klaus doesn't allow me up on the bed that much anymore, but I figure today will be an exception. And even if it isn't, I'm still getting up on that bed to see what's going on. Tentatively, I test the idea by putting just my paws up. Klaus says nothing; he is on the bed, too, sitting next to Momma, who looks exhausted. But lying against her chest is something so small, so fragile, I immediately go on the defensive. No one—and that even goes for Poe—will harm one single hair atop the new addition's head.

I look towards the foot of the bed, and that's where I see Amelia and her little human. Both have smiles on their faces as they watch Jada and Klaus.

*"See, Dali, I told you he would be a handful. You already want to protect their bundle. That's just what you do. Protect those three with your life, Dali girl."*

I huff out my answer, and when Amelia has stayed for as long as she can, she disappears. Then, it's just the five of us. I wonder why Momma and Klaus can't see Amelia and little Nico, but Poe explained to me that humans can't see those who've passed on to the next life. Not unless they are sensitive and open to the idea.

"Gorgeous, you did good."

"You think?"

"I know."

Momma looks over to me and smiles. "Dali, come and have a closer look at your brother, Vidor. Isn't he everything?"

She tilts the baby forward so I can get a closer

look, and I have to agree. The little male human is everything.

"Jada, we need to get him cleaned up and have him looked at."

"I know, just want to hold him a little bit longer."

"All right, gorgeous." Klaus kisses the top of Momma's head and whispers, "I love you, Jada Aegir."

"Love you, too, Klaus."

Our family has just received another root. New life. And as Vidor's branches cling to his human parents, I think to myself, *Vidor's roots are planted deep. Deep into the souls of two people who were always meant to share their hearts.* I listen carefully to each human's heartbeat. They are synced and in tune. A true merging of souls as their hearts beat as one.

THANK YOU FOR READING

If you enjoyed Affinity, please be sure to sign up for my newsletter and stay informed on all new release information as it becomes available: https://www.subscribepage.com/NewslettersignupTigriseden

---

If you like my books, please be sure to join my reader group where I share covers and excerpts. Eden's Den is always looking for more members: https://www.facebook.com/groups/EdensDen/

UP NEXT: CONSUMED

Read an excerpt from Consumed, a Paranormal Set in the Soulful Hearts World.

Read Consumed Today!

---

**Consumed Synopsis**

As a woman in a man's world, firefighter, Abrihet has always had to push just a little bit harder, prove just a little bit more. But her special gifts don't make that any easier. Fire isn't something she fights, it's something she controls. And that's a secret that she doesn't want getting out. However, when a routine rescue goes south quickly, and Abrihet is literally pulled from the flames into hell, she has no choice but to accept the hand she's been dealt.

As the heir to the throne of Wraith, Fire Demon Bael was raised to hate Nefas—half-demon, half-human hybrids. But when he's sent to watch and pass judgment on the daughter of one of his Enforcers, he finds something wholly unexpected. She's not an abomination. Actually, she might just be his salvation. The challenge will be getting her to accept him and his ways, because as the heir, his world is darker than most.

Despite the odds stacked against them and the unusual circumstances of their meeting, Bael and Abrihet must learn to trust each other and work together. If they don't, it could mean death for one or both of them. Luckily, their connection is strong, and attraction burns bright. But is the light they share something they can use to fight those who oppose them, or will it consume them both?

Paranormal Romance with Fire Demons.

## Read Consumed Today!

# UP NEXT: CONSUMED

Fire licked up the sides of the wall. The flames had long since destroyed most of what was left of the building. The smoke would cloud anyone's ability to see. But not Abrihet's. She remained un-affected. Even in the uniform she was forced to wear and the helmet shield covering her face, her vision was clear. Playing along was the only way the others would keep from guessing her secret. Fire had no effect on her. Never had. The protective gear she wore made things more difficult to navigate as sweat dropped into her eyes. She could hear the screams. Each one distinct and different. There were at least three more people in the building. Abrihet was going to get in a shit-ton of trouble for going in after them without backup. Her captain had already warned her on more than one occasion about putting herself in harm's way. He thought she was just trying to be "one of the guys." It was the furthest thing from the truth.

She wasn't trying to prove anything. Though, if she could take the suit off without bringing attention to herself, she would. She needed to get to the three innocent people trapped behind a door that was red-hot in a building currently going up in flames.

Abrihet knew she was different. It was kind of hard to miss. When she'd realized fire had no effect on her, she'd tested it out in stages. She was resistant to even the hottest of fires. Her skin didn't melt on contact, and there were times the flames themselves spoke to her. But, tonight, all she could hear were the cries of the three people trapped behind the door. None of the other guys had been able to get up through the hole that was created in the ceiling that led to the second floor. It left only her. She had to be the one to go. She had to try to save the people.

Although the guys had said they couldn't hear any screams, Abrihet could. They'd entered through the back door, but when half of the second floor collapsed, it had left them with very few options. She'd heard the call for help all too clearly. Even if the guys couldn't hear them, she could, and they weren't going to tell her she couldn't go up there. It was their job to save people.

Kole was going to kick her ass, and Samson was going to give her the cold shoulder for a week for pulling this stunt. Abrihet could picture him tugging on the ends of his brown hair with one hand as the other rested on his hip. Samson was quite the character. And friends with her brother and Kole Brandt, who worked over at Station 58. *Fuck. I'm so screwed.* Yeah, she was. Because Samson didn't know how to keep his mouth shut. She'd bet her last *Double Stuf Oreo* cookie that the man was seconds away from ratting her out. Something he frequently did. She loved him, and Kole, and they kept an eye on her for her brother, Keenan, who was still an active member of the military. Kole and Samson were no longer active duty.

She saw the support beam ahead, covered in flames. It was bending to the fire's will as it protested and groaned. She had maybe a couple of minutes' tops to get in and get the people out. Abrihet walked right through the blaze, her jacket singeing as the fire licked at her. But as she pushed through, the fire parted, allowing her to pass. If she didn't know any better, she'd have said she was in complete control.

She didn't have time to test that theory.

Bad shit would happen if she did. Every time she tried to control the fire, a mysterious man popped up and started speaking to her in a language she knew she shouldn't understand, but did. The look in his eyes told her he was upset by her knowledge of what she could do, and he warned her to stop lest there be consequences. She could talk herself into thinking it was some sort of dream. But that would mean her entire life was a dream. Because no human could control fire. Not really. Maybe in the movies, but in real life… No. That just didn't happen.

But she wasn't dreaming. This was real. And she

could control the element. Therefore, the mysterious man must exist, as well. And she *should* heed his warnings. As it was, she had to downplay her abilities, constantly lying to her fellow teammates. Once, she'd literally been caught with her hand in fire. When confronted by one of the guys, who was clearly confused, she'd confessed to having a fascination with flames. Somehow, she'd convinced him that her hand wasn't in the fire, only close to it. But still, he asked questions. Like, why wasn't her hand covered in blisters, or at the very least red?

Her only response to that was that she'd covered her hand in fire retardant gel. He'd accepted her answer after some convincing. Whether he actually believed her or not was an entirely different question.

Abrihet was right up on the door now and called out to those trapped. "Can you hear me? I'm going to get you out of there, but I need you to stay calm, okay?"

More screams, and this time, the urgency in the tone ripped through her. Pushing through the door, Abrihet made sure not to grab the handle. Her gloves were heat resistant, but she wasn't going to chance it. She needed this to be a mistake-free rescue. As the door opened, Abrihet froze in shock. There wasn't anyone in the room. Not one single person.

"Hello?" she called. "Anybody in here?" She knew there wasn't because she could see clearly. But she called out anyway, hoping she was wrong.

Again, no one answered. She was in the room alone. The roar of the flames was at her back as it rushed the room and engulfed her. *Shit.* She was hearing voices again. Could it be the flames calling out to her? Abrihet didn't want to get caught up in the voices again. Last time that happened, she lost her best friend. *Sara.*

They'd been playing in the woods. Every summer, Sara's mom would take them camping. That year, the forest had caught fire. It had been a freak accident. Trapped in the flames, the girls had screamed for help, but no one came. That was when Abrihet had first heard the voices. She'd been too young to understand what was happening. The flames began to speak, guiding her, pulling her towards safety and freedom. She still wasn't sure what would have happened if no one had found her when all was said and done, but she'd listened to those voices, and in her eight-year-old mind, she'd assumed that if she could walk through the flames, so could Sara. Her friend had died from third-degree burns and smoke inhalation.

She knew now: she had a gift, and she needed to

use that gift for good. *I couldn't be there for Sara, but I can be there for others.* It was her fault that Sara was dead. It was her responsibility to atone for that. Abrihet shook the memory from her mind as she began to slowly back out of the room. Each step was a practiced movement. One wrong move and the floor could collapse. No sooner had the thought crossed her mind, she was falling. She was impervious to fire, but broken bones…not so much.

Her left arm bent at an awkward angle when she smashed into a support beam on her way down, causing Abrihet's vision to blur from pain as she tried to grab hold of anything that would stop or possibly break her fall with her good hand. The landing was no better, maybe worse, and the sharp pain that radiated from her ankle all the way to her hip caused her to cry out. *I'm so screwed.* As the agony coursed through her body, the building began to crumble and collapse around her. There were people shouting. Different people, not the phantoms from before. Her team, she was sure of it. In front of her, a figure began to take shape, but barely. The one thing she could see clearly was the eyes. A black void filled with hatred.

A moment of stark fear coursed through her, tingling down her spine, but it quickly evaporated as she felt hands tug on her shoulders but not before the dark figure took hold of her legs. It was like a tug of war. One end pulled against the other, and as the building continued to crumble, she heard someone shout her name as she was pulled back into the fire.

---

Read Consumed Today!

ABOUT THE AUTHOR

Tigris Eden is a military brat who's done her fair share of traveling, thanks to her Army father. She's married to the infamous LL and has three boys. She currently resides in Houston and is actively seeking a book-buddy for the end of the world.

www.tigriseden.com

facebook.com/TigrisEdenAuthor

twitter.com/tigris_eden

instagram.com/tigriseden

OTHER TITLES BY TIGRIS EDEN

**Shadow Unit Series Paranormal Romance**

Enslaved in Shadows Book

Burned in Shadows Book

Bonded in Shadows *Novella*

Redeemed in Shadows

Awakened in Shadows

The Black Prince

Inferis

---

**Arctic Wolves Series Paranormal Romance**

Arctic Bound

The Reaping

Dire Cravings

---

**Southern Contemporary Romance**

A Slow Burn

Give and Take

Until Her

---

**V Vices Series**

Diamond: Beyond the Red Door

---

**Soulful Hearts Series**

Affinity

Consumed

---

**Standalones**

After Hours: Ryan and Bennett - Available on Radish

In the Cover of Night

A Game of Hearts

## PRAISE FOR THE SHADOW UNIT SERIES

"The Shadow Unit Series is an edge of your seat thrill ride full of steamy romance, conspiracy and best of all, hot shifters. A great series for any lover of the genre."

— *AUTHOR S. CU'ANAM POLICAR*

"This was one of the best 2nd in a series books I think I have ever read. I have been waiting to see what happened with Jes and Draven, the hotness that is Royce and Ronin. Great Follow up. Great writing, can't wait till the others come out!"

— *TKA3NME*

## PRAISE FOR THE SHADOW UNIT SERIES

"Just when you think happily ever after there is another twist in the story that keeps you turning the page."

— *1SAFELADY*

"The Shadow Unit Series is intense, gritty and HOT HOT HOT!!!"

— *VIKI SLOBODA*

"Intrigue, love and action make an irresistible read."

— *VONDETTA CARTER*

"Once you start reading them you can't put them down until you're finished. Then you are anxiously waiting for the next."

— *BARB A.*

"Shadow Unit Series is an emotional, raw, sexy, action packed paranormal fabulousness that sucks you in from page one. You will cry, laugh, and blush throughout the series and burn for more."

— *INDY BOOK FAIRY*

"Hunky men, steamy scenes, romance and a touch of the paranormal. What more can you ask for? It's all here in the Shadow Unit."

— *JENNIFER BALLAM*

"The Shadow Unit series is an edge of your seat mix of adventure and romance that will leave the readers wanting more!"

— *TY LANGSTON, AUTHOR OF DECADENT DREAMS*

PRAISE FOR ARCTIC BOUND

"Arctic Bound is meltingly passionate and explosively sexy! Ms. Eden brings us an amazing story. Arctic Bound kept me guessing! Doesn't happen often but I was stunned speechless a few times with plot twists I never saw coming."

— BITTEN BY LOVE REVIEWS

"I enjoyed Arctic Bound because of the heroine, she was no one's push over. She was a fighter. There was passion, mystery and all kinds of paranormal creatures."

— *DEBRA CROSBY*

## PRAISE FOR ARCTIC BOUND

"Do you want dark and brooding? Check. Do you want a heroine with a troubled past? Check. Do you want the leads to not be physically perfect? Partial check. Do you want your paranormal favorites in one place? Huge Check!"

— *JENNY*

"I love Tigris Eden as an author and here's why, she puts everything I want in a book without it being too much. I am a huge fan of adding diversity into books and Tigris delivers."

— *REESE'S BOOK REVIEWS*

"The well-orchestrated events of this romance keep readers on the edge of their seats and ensure that the readers want to know everything. I was completely bewitched by the Arctic Wolves and their fascinating world and I can't wait to read the next one."

— *EVAMPIRE*

PRAISE FOR DIAMOND

"My first book from this author and most certainly not my last. There are a lot of books available that claim to be dystopian with dark undertones but this book just knocked me for six! I wasn't quite sure what to expect but whatever it was it most certainly wasn't this. I read the synopsis and thought alrighty then futuristic sci fi with a mysterious heroine and the stereo typical alpha male. Can I state here and now that this book seems to have a life of its own and if it's a romance you seek then perhaps you will scream but if you want to get knocked on your (no doubt) shapely behind then this book deserves to be read!"

— *MARTA COX*

Made in the USA
Coppell, TX
05 March 2026

72911930R00114